Kirkus Review (October 1, 2009)

Five-year-old Marta Carney's murder changes the lives of three Depression-era Chicago teens. Fred and Maizy are from the poorer neighborhoods, but both attract the attention of Zane, a pampered preacher's son. When Zane's father becomes gravely ill, the teens uncover his dark secret. Stillerman struggles with her historical setting, failing to bring it to life, though some of her language choices try to help it along. Maizy's rape is somehow both brutal and understated; in keeping with the sensibilities of the times, Maizy is held responsible for Zane's actions and even naïvely believes she and Zane will achieve happiness. Despite a somewhat endearing first crush on Maizy, Fred's persona is otherwise bland, and he's easily overlooked. Although she tells the story from three different viewpoints, the author never differentiates the voices enough to make the device work. While the boys' forensic knowledge appears incongruous with the era, this is only a minor flaw among many. Kenmore Street may have seen something awful, but the narrative is a dead end. (Historical fiction. YA)

Something
TERRIBLE
HAPPENED ON
KENMORE

Dedication

To my husband, Jack, a constant source of love and support, who is always in the wings, cheering me on.

And to my readers, the young people who are the hope of our world.

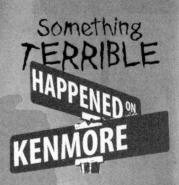

Something
TERRIBLE
HAPPENED ON
KENMORE

MARCI STILLERMAN

WestSide Books
Lodi, New Jersey

Published by WestSide Books
60 Industrial Road
Lodi, NJ 07644
973-458-0485
Fax: 973-458-5289

Library of Congress Control Number: 2009930788

International Standard Book Number: 978-1-934813-11-9
School ISBN: 978-1-934813-27-0
Cover illustration by Michael Morgenstern
Cover design by David Lemanowicz
Interior design by David Lemanowicz

Printed in the United States of America
10 9 8 7 6 5 4 3 2 1

First Edition

Something
TERRIBLE
HAPPENED ON
KENMORE

CHAPTER 1

Fred

Something terrible happened on Kenmore, only a couple weeks after me and my ma moved here. On the first day of June, a little girl from this street was murdered. It's three weeks later, and there are stories about it in the *Chicago Tribune* every day.

The girl's name was Marta Carney, only five years old. Her folks, Anna and Josef Carney, came from Poland like my pa did. They changed their name from Karnofsky when they came to America. First they lived in a small town in Kentucky, Libra, the paper said, then they moved to Chicago to live in a big city. It wasn't a lucky move for them.

The story in the paper said Marta's body was found in Lake Michigan, only a few blocks from here. The right hand was cut off. The killer is unknown and the hand is missing. Maybe if the hand shows up, they'll have a clue to the killer.

I feel sorry for the girl's folks. I know what it's like for someone you love to get killed.

We always lived in Chicago, and so far it hasn't been

lucky for us, either. My pa was shot a year ago last Christmas. After he got killed, Ma and I had to live in one room in a hotel before she got a housekeeper job and we moved to this apartment. It's a lot like the street we lived on when Pa had his hardware store. The apartment is small and stuffy but it's better than the hotel.

There are trees and houses on Kenmore—a few walk-up apartment buildings like the one we live in—and back-yards, and little kids playing outside.

The dead girl was one of those kids, playing with her friends until just a few weeks ago.

It's summer vacation, so there are kids my age around, too, sitting on their stoops, hitting balls in the alley, listening to music, or just fooling around.

Ma says keep out of trouble. Watch who you hang out with.

So far, I don't know anyone to hang with. I'm trying to get a job to help out with expenses but so far, no luck. Seems all the summer jobs for kids were taken before school let out for vacation.

I'm sitting on the curb in front of our building one sweltering afternoon, trying to get a breeze, when these three guys pass by on their bikes. They look about my age, sixteen or seventeen. At the end of the block, they turn around and bike back to where I'm sitting.

"You new here?" the one with shoes on asks.

"Yeah," I say. They park their bikes and we look each other over. They're ordinary guys, like kids at the hotel. Shoes is the shortest, with light brown hair, cut short in back, longer on top. The others have buzz cuts like me, and stubble faces showing boredom. We're all wearing the same kind of duds—tee shirts and jeans—like they're from the same bin at the Goodwill.

I'm more like Shoes than the others I guess, not as tall as the big guy, and not as muscled. And I got no stubble— hardly any beard yet, being light skinned. Guess I take after my Polish pa, same washed-out blue eyes. Ma calls them sky blue, which I hate, but that's a ma for you.

"Whatcher name?" Shoes asks. He's the only one talking, like he's in charge.

"Fred Fink," I say, expecting the kind of wisecrack my name usually gets. Doesn't happen.

Shoes's name is Zane. He points to the others, Marko and Chip. They nod.

"You read about the murder 'a that kid?" Zane asks. Marko has lit up a butt he took out of his pocket. Chip offers around a pack of Juicy Fruit.

I take a stick and say thanks. "Yeah, I been reading about the murder," I say. "They get the killer yet?"

"Nah," Zane says. "But we got the missing hand."

"No way," I say.

"Yeah. Marko was looking for bottles and found it at the bottom of a trash barrel."

"So didja give it to the cops?"

"You crazy?" Marko says. "Why'd we do that?"

"And have them pin it on us?" Chip says. "We're in trouble with the cops as it is, Marko and me— shoplifting."

"It's got the ring on the finger, like her pa said. And you know what else?" Marko says. "Some hair from the killer is in her fist, like she pulled it outta his head when he grabbed her. It's why the killer had to get rid of the hand. It's evidence. When they nab him, they can match up his hair with the hair in the hand."

"We're the only ones know about the hair. Nobody else ever saw that hand," Zane says, smirking like it's the secret of the universe.

I'm thinking maybe it's a crime not to turn in the hand, but I'm not saying so. Don't want them banging on me first time I talk to them.

So instead I ask where they're keeping it.

"Why should we tell you? You could squeal and we'd have to kill you."

"I don't squeal," I say. I'm insulted they'd think that.

"Well, okay, then," Zane says. "I'll show you." He acts like it's his claim to fame, having a murdered kid's hand, something no one but him and his pals know about.

I get on my bike and follow them down the street to an empty lot. Behind a rotted-out billboard is this old, broken-down construction shed, windows mostly busted out. Pretty much of a wreck, but the door is painted blue with Z's in black.

" 'Z's' means me," Zane says, as if I wouldn't've known. "It's private. Like our private hangout. Right?"

The guys shrug.

"If you say so," Marko says.

"Only me and my guys got keys," Zane says.

Inside is a couch and some chairs, a table—the kind of stuff people put out on their curbs for the garbage man to pick up. There's a couple of bottles holding candles on the table. Some cabinets in a corner. There's no electricity. But not a bad place to hang out. I don't ask, but I suspect they got some booze or cigarettes stashed in the cabinets, and maybe beer. Probably bring their girls here to make out.

I ask if this is where the hand's buried.

"Maybe," Zane says. I notice Marko and Chip eyeing one of the loose boards on the floor. I tell myself, *that's where it is.* "Wanna see it?"

Nah, I don't. I'll take their word for it.

Zane brings bottles of Coke.

"Make yourself at home," he says, and we sit and gab. I tell them about living in the hotel—how the halls stink of piss and booze, and how you gotta lock yourself in at night or they'll steal anything you've got.

"They got gangs there?" Marko wants to know.

I tell them the Gaylords come around. I don't know that for sure, but it's possible.

They're impressed.

"You got a girl?"

I tell them I just moved here. Don't know any girls.

"Wanna meet Maizy?" Zane asks.

"Who's she?" I ask.

"Someone you can make it with. We all did," Marko says, grinning like a cat that just swallowed a pail of tuna. "Z fixed it."

"Yeah," I say. "Okay. Some other time."

"Now," Zane says. "Let's go. She's real easy. You'll see."

We leave the shack, tossing our empty bottles on the ground and get on our bikes.

"Come again," Zane says, closing the door. "You're always welcome at Z's."

CHAPTER 2

Fred

I got on my bike and followed them to Maizy's house. She was in her yard, a small fenced-in space with a few clumps of grass, a couple trees. She was swinging on an inner tube, kicking rocks outta her way. She was fat. Real pretty face, like a blue-eyed, yellow-haired doll. Wearing a tight red shirt and a pair of shorts, showing a tire of fat in between. Real friendly smile.

"Say hi to Maizy," Zane said, and the three of them took off, not staying to see if the introduction took. I nodded and gave her a hand flick. I didn't know, was I supposed to hang around? After a minute thinking it over, I was off in the opposite direction.

❖

Later that afternoon, I biked back to her place. Like a jerk, I'd left too fast to do whatever was expected of me, by the guys or by her. She was sitting on her front stoop, holding a bottle of Coke.

"Remember me?"

She did, and we gabbed for a while, me leaning on my bike. I told her I just moved here, and about the hotel, how the elevator never worked, and how you had to hike up seven floors every time you had to go to the toilet. How a million kids raced around in the halls all day, and peed in the stairwells. Not a great place to live, but how it was there or the street after my pa got shot.

"Dead?"

"Yeah. Things happen." I was not going to talk about it. I'd said enough already.

"Well, welcome to the neighborhood," she said.

I sat on the stoop next to her and we jawed some about the murder.

"I cried when I heard about that poor little kid," she said. "Anna Carney's the ma. They live on this street. She's young. They're from the mountains where they hitch up early. Must be awful for her. You don't ever get over something like that."

"Yeah, I read all about it."

We sipped our Cokes for a while.

"Awful hot," I said, trying to make small talk.

"Want to come in my basement and cool off?" she said.

It was cool in there all right, and bare. One piece of furniture, a couch leaking its stuffing. We flopped down and with no discussion, like it was expected, I put my hands on her titties and then down her shorts. I never done that to a girl before, never had the chance, or to tell the truth, the inclination, but it seemed expected. She didn't push me away. I got on top of her, and I liked the feel of all that soft fat against me. It excited me. I rubbed against her, and quick as a flash, I exploded. Leaked on her legs, wet my shorts and hers, too. I was hot with embarrassment.

I knew the guys were going to ask me if I made it. That's why they brought me there. Did what happened count as making it, I wondered? If Maizy told that I didn't even get inside her, I'd be done for.

She laughed, not mean but happy, like she was having a good time, so I felt okay, and not put down. She grabbed a handful of tissues and gave me some, and we both mopped off. We hugged. She went upstairs and brought down some cold Coke. We lit up a cigarette I got from the janitor at the hotel for helping with the garbage, my first and only, and the way she coughed and sputtered, I could tell it was hers, too.

"What about them guys I was with?" I asked.

"They're okay."

"You do it with all of them?"

She laughed. "We fool around some. They're just kids. Don't mean no harm."

"But why d'you let them?"

She shrugged. "So they'll like me. 'Specially Zane."

"Shoes."

" 'Shoes'?" Then she got it. "Yeah. That's Zane."

"So that's how you get boyfriends?"

"They're not boyfriends. Just friends, like in not enemies."

I was thinking, *I don't like her fooling around with those guys, but I got no right to tell her what to do. She's not my girlfriend, and I'm not about to hitch up with a girl.*

15

Anyhow, why should I care? Just because she was nice to me, don't mean I gotta worry about her.

CHAPTER 3

Fred

I spend all next day doing a bunch of errands for Ma—shopping at the grocery store, taking clothes to the laundry, buying light bulbs, all stuff she needs doing because she works all day. When she gets home, I surprise her by having supper ready—hot dogs, coleslaw, fries, and some ice-cold Cokes. I tell her I'll do the cooking all summer—she's just got to say what and how. She gives me a big hug. I tell her it's the least I can do to help out since I haven't been able to get a job so far.

After we eat and she's soaking her feet and dozing by the radio, I decide I'll bike over to Maizy's. Seems like the right thing to do after her being so nice to me.

She's sitting on her step, sucking a grape Popsicle. She gives me a purple smile. She's wearing coveralls. Her bare round arms look soft and, I tell myself, kinda sweet, though sweet's not a word I'd ever say aloud.

"Hey, there," she says.

"Just passing by," I say, not wanting to give her the idea I came to see her.

"Want a Coke?"

I brake the bike and flop down on the step next to her. "Got a beer?"

"I guess." Her look says *you drink beer?* But she shrugs her shoulders and goes in the house to get it.

It's not dark yet, but the light's seeping outta the sky and the street lamps have already come on. It's hot, but there's a breeze; smells wet, like the lake. Lake Michigan is just a couple blocks away.

I really dig the lake. I make up my mind to bike over there real soon and spend some hours on the rocks, maybe go fishing. My pa took me fishing off the pier on Twelfth Street a couple times. I still have his rod and rusty old bait box.

When Maizy comes back with the beer, I push over near her on the step so my bare arm touches hers, which is cool and solid, and salted with freckles. I feel good, sitting there with her, swigging the beer like I was used to having a bottle a beer on a summer evening. Little kids on roller skates streak by. Two girls up the street are jumping rope, and a guy and girl are making out on the steps next door. Music spills out of open windows, men holler at their wives, a baby cries, and barbecue smells smoke up the air. I'm happier'n I've been in a long time.

We don't talk for a while, she chewing purple ice and me swigging beer from the brown bottle.

"There's this old shack," I say, "few streets north of here. Those guys brought me to meet you use it as a kind of hangout. They call it Z's. Supposed to be a secret."

"I never tell secrets," she says.

"Yeah. I got a gut feeling you don't. Well, it's not a bad place to do private stuff."

"What kind of stuff?"

I'm not telling what's buried in the floor.

"I guess they smoke some. Maybe do some drinking."

"You?"

"Yeah, if I get it." I'm not about to admit I'm nearly a virgin when it comes to booze. "My ma'd kill me. How 'bout you?"

"Ummmm . . ." Like she don't want to admit she's a square like me.

"I'm pissed about the gun someone hid in the shack," I say.

"Snatch it when no one's there. Dump it."

"They'd know who took it."

"Yeah. Well, they'll never use it. I know the guys around here. Hard crust outside, but mush inside."

"I think they could use it. Zane isn't mush. He's real intense."

She gives me a look I don't get. I think she's got feelings for Zane.

It's getting dark, and a dusty wind rattles the gutter trash.

"Wanna come in for a while?" she asks. "I gotta get supper started before Pa comes home. He gets real mad if supper's late. You can listen to the comics on the radio with Joey."

"Joey?"

"My little brother. I take care of him."

"Why don't he come out?"

She shrugs. "He doesn't want to miss his program."

My interest in going inside the house with Maizy melts like ice cream on a hot stove when I hear there's a Joey.

"Thanks. But I gotta go."

CHAPTER 4

Maizy

One hot afternoon in June, Maizy'd set out to buy groceries. On her way through the park, she had to pee. There was a public lavatory in the park, but just her luck the ladies' room was closed for repair. She peeked into the grimy window of the men's. If it was empty, she'd use it.

But it wasn't. Through the window, she saw a man and a little girl. He had his hand on her shoulder. He seemed to be talking to her, but she wasn't looking at him. She was looking at the floor. Maizy couldn't see her eyes.

She'd seen the man before, here in the park, watching the kids play, and walking on Kenmore. She'd been sitting on her step one morning and caught him staring at her from across the street. No one ever looked at her the way he did, as if his eyes could peel her like a banana. Even at that distance, she could see he had unusual eyes, steady and black as tar. If you got caught in them, it would be hard to pull away. She'd looked away just in time.

The little girl with him in the men's bathroom could be any one of the kids in the neighborhood.

What were they doing there, the man and the little girl?

21

The man looked up and Maizy was sure he saw her. He'd recognize her from being on Kenmore. She took off, running. Scared. If he knew she saw him and he was doing something bad, he could get her.

❖

All that day, she couldn't get it off her mind—that guy, a man in a suit, in the men's lavatory with a little girl. Maybe it was all right. There could be a reason—but she didn't know. She just didn't know.

If something happened after she left, well, how would she know?

But she was sure she'd never forget his face.

She couldn't stop thinking about it while she was cleaning the house and cutting up vegetables for stew.

The man'd seen her. She knew he did. A man like that could come after her if he thought she'd turned him in, or his friends could. She'd keep mum about him and what she saw.

Funny that that man in the business suit would stare so hard at her, with his magnet eyes, like he'd never seen a fat girl with big boobs before. She'd wanted to tell somebody about seeing him in the men's lav in the park, but who? The police wouldn't believe her, and what could she tell them anyway? She'd never tell her pa. He'd say mind your own business. Not her girlfriends, either. They wouldn't know any more what to do than she did.

Maizy didn't see her girlfriends much. It was summer vacation and they were mostly working. She missed talking to them, even though all they ever talked about was boys.

"You got a boyfriend yet, Maizy?" they wanted to know. They had boyfriends, lots of them, different ones every week. If Maizy could have had a boyfriend, it would have to be Zane. For her, it had never been anyone else. Not since they were little kids and his nanny brought him from across Sheridan Road, where the rich people lived, to the playground near Kenmore. She'd loved the skinny little boy since she was six and he was five. He had clean yellow hair, clean white teeth, clean fingernails, and every morning, clean clothes. Different from the neighborhood kids, whose moms sent them to the park to play in any kind of getup— their pa's old shirts, sometimes the pajamas they slept in. No one around to wipe their noses or pick them up if they fell down. No nannies, just one ma watching her kids and the neighbors', all at the same time.

In those days, and all through most of grammar school, Maizy was just another kid to Zane. He didn't know he was special to her.

When she was eleven, she'd all of a sudden gotten these amazing boobs. That was when Zane first noticed her. When they were in high school, she let him get her into a corner in the schoolyard and feel her up. Then she let his friends. She thought it'd please him.

"You're a fool to let them," her girlfriend said.

"I don't care. It don't hurt me."

It didn't hurt like being called names or being laughed at, and it made the boys like her. If you're thin and pretty, you don't need to do anything to get boys to like you.

23

❖

A few days after Maizy saw the girl and the man in the lav, she read in the paper about how a little girl on Kenmore, Marta Carney, was killed. Was it Marta she'd seen in the lav with the man? Was that man—the same one she'd seen on Kenmore—the killer? Maizy was terrified. The guy had seen her; he knew she saw him. He could kill her to make sure she wouldn't tell. Now she watched for him all the time, and she kept watching wherever she went.

She'd never forget his face.

❖

Anna Carney, Marta's mother, came to the playground often that summer. Maizy knew her from her pictures in the paper. She sat on a bench and watched the children play. Why did she come? It must be awful sad for her, now that Marta was not playing in the sandbox or on the slides anymore. Maizy sat down on the bench near Anna one morning. She imagined how they must look sitting there, two girls among the mothers, herself fat and dressed to let as much air reach her body as possible but still sweating, with her long blond hair in a tight braid down her back. And there was Anna, thin as a toothpick and as shapeless, her sad pale face all eyes, watching the children. Her colorless hair was pinned back with clips, like she just wanted to get it out of the way. She dressed in washed-out skirts and blouses that needed ironing. Maizy thought she looked like a neglected orphan or a girl who didn't eat enough.

"Hot, isn't it?" Maizy said, trying to get a conversation going.

Anna didn't answer.

"I'm sorry about your little girl."

Anna nodded.

After that, when both were at the playground, they always sat on the same bench, not talking about anything, but somehow companionable.

Maizy knew Anna was mourning. She wished there was some way she could get her little girl back for her.

On a hot afternoon toward the end of July, Maizy was on her way to the grocery to buy bread when a car pulled up alongside her. A horn honked, startling her.

"Hey, Maizy, want a ride?"

It was Zane. She hadn't talked to him since school was out for the summer, though she'd seen him on Kenmore with his buddies. When he was with the guys, he was likely to pass by and not see her, like she was a piece of chewed gum lying in the gutter. Hurt her some, but when guys were together, they never wanted to talk to an unpopular girl like her.

"Where'd you get the neat car?"

She bent down, leaned in the open window. It was a white Chevy, not new, but real nice.

"My dad gave it to me when I turned sixteen. Like it?"

He'd had a birthday. If she'd known, she could've sent a card.

"Sure."

She knew she looked sweaty; she always sweated. She should've fixed herself up when she left the house. Never know who you'll see. Should've changed her shorts for a clean pair, put on one of her pa's shirts she'd just washed and ironed for him. He had a turquoise blue, fit her real good, the color matched her eyes.

"I really gotta get home," she said. "I watch my brother Joey when Pa's at work."

"Come for a ride. Then I'll take you home."

"Well, maybe for a little while." If she refused, he might never ask her again. He reached over and opened the door.

"Good," Zane said. "I been wantin' to show you my car."

Sitting beside him on the hot leather seat, she thought of the last time he'd pressed his skinny body against her in the schoolyard and rubbed himself on her. She'd wanted to put her arms around him, but his hands were jammed in his pockets and she knew he wouldn't've wanted her to hold him with all the guys watching. So she kept her arms at her sides, her palms pressed against the rough stone of the school building. And didn't want it to be over.

With Zane, it was different from the other boys. He didn't smell like hair goo and breakfast. He had a certain Zane smell she loved, soapy and clean clothes. Thinking about those days in school, she felt something was lost, like the string had broken on one of those helium balloons and it was gone for good. She wouldn't be going back to school. Pa said so.

It'd be okay to go for a ride with Zane, she decided. Joey'd be listening to cowboy shows on the radio—wouldn't notice if she was gone for ten minutes or an hour.

"None of the other guys got a car," she said, running her hand over the leather seat.

"Nope."

"You got a great pa."

"Yeah."

The car took off with a *whoosh*.

Both of them had only a pa, no ma. They'd once talked about this. But it wasn't the same thing. Zane's father was a minister and they lived in the rectory of his church on the lakefront, just a few blocks from Kenmore, but real different. Like the other rich people living on Sheridan Road, the minister had a housekeeper who took care of them, cooked and cleaned. And Zane had a nanny when he was little—after his mother died.

Maizy's pa was a plain working man, a maintenance worker for the city, the kind where your clothes got dirty, where there was dirt under your nails and in the creases of your skin. Maizy was eight when her mama died. A big girl already, Pa said, old enough to take care of Joey, the baby. She could bring him to daycare and pick him up after school, and during summer vacation, she would take care of him all day. There was no nanny to take Joey to the playground or bathe him and feed him. But Joey was a good boy. Too good, Maizy thought. He didn't talk a lot, and as long as you let him listen to his favorite radio shows and draw in his coloring books with Indians and cowboys, he was no bother at all.

"You've got a great pa, Zane," Maizy repeated, wanting to say something. "He's really nice to you, giving you a car and all."

"Yeah. Well, I'm supposed to do what he says. He don't like me coming here."

"But all your friends're here."

"Yeah, I know that. But he don't like it. Wants me to be with the church kids. Go to Bible School, sing in the choir." Zane snickered. "Bunch a fools. Since that little girl got wasted, he's all over me to stay away from here. Says perverts hang out in this kind of neighborhood."

"Yeah, I know. I'm scared to go out, 'specially at night."

"Why're you scared?" Zane said. "No one's gonna come after you."

She knew he meant because she was fat. Perverts never went for fat girls. But Zane didn't know the man had seen her. Knew who she was. Could want her out of the way because she'd seen him with Marta. She was in danger.

"We don't have to talk about it, do we?" He put his hand on her thigh, just where her shorts ended. "You look good, Maizy. Haven't changed since I saw you last."

"Still fat, you mean?" She laughed, looked at his hand on her leg. Still had clean fingernails, like when he was little.

"Yeah, well, I don't mind a little flesh. You're a pretty girl, Maizy."

He took his blue eyes off the street to look her up and down.

His touch, his look stirred up feelings in her. It was like her blood heated up and made her stomach ache, but in a good way. Excited. She felt down there like she'd never felt before. She stared out the window to calm herself. His hand was on her crotch, his fingers moving inside her shorts. She couldn't suppress a gasp. She bit down on her lower lip.

"Like that, don't you?"

She nodded. She hugged his arm against her side. Sweat dripped down her face, stinging her eyes.

"Let go my arm." He laughed. "I gotta make a turn just ahead. Don't worry. We're not through yet. I got a plan."

"I should get home," she said, clearing her throat so her voice wouldn't shake.

At the end of the block, he turned the car into an empty lot. He drove a short distance across rutted ground to a crumbling billboard that half hid a construction shack. He leaned over her and opened her door. They got out and walked to the shack.

The shack's windows were broken out, but there were three good steps leading up to a nice door, painted blue. It had a shiny brass knob, and when he unlocked it, it opened on good hinges. In strong letters across the top, Z's was printed in black.

"Whose shack is it?" she asked.

"Mine. It's a secret hangout. I found it, so I'm in charge."

She didn't let on she knew about Z's, never even said Fred Fink told her about it. That might spoil it for Zane, knowing she already knew of it.

"Who else knows? Those pals of yours? Chip, Marko and them?"

"Yeah. You know them?" He knew she did. He'd sent all of them to her in the schoolyard.

Maizy followed him up the steps into a long narrow room. The sun hung on the dust motes in the air like a spider hangs on his web. There was a couch and some chairs, a card table on rickety legs, and a bunch of big floor pillows. On a ledge running along a side of the room was a lantern, some candles, safety matches in a blue cup, and a padlocked box. One of the floorboards was loose, but it was an okay place for a hangout.

He lit one of the candles and set it in its own wax on the table.

"Well?"

"It's nice. You could live here."

"There's a toilet behind the curtain. Don't get any ideas about using it unless you intend to clean it up."

Zane selected a thin key from a chain he took out of his pocket, opened the lock on the metal box, took out a thin brown tube, and relocked the box.

"Sit down." He indicated the sofa and applied a match to the hand-rolled cigarette. He got two glasses out of a cabinet and a small bottle, and poured some clear liquid into the glasses.

"You drink booze here?" Maizy asked. "Aren't you scared you'll get caught?"

"Who'll come snooping? We don't bring anyone here we don't trust." He looked at her hard.

He knew he could trust her.

He lit the cigarette and handed it to her. Maizy giggled.

"I never smoked before."

"Well, you gotta start sometime." She coughed and he laughed.

"Keep going," he said. "It gets better. Try this." He handed her one of the glasses. "Do what I do."

He put the other glass to his lips and swallowed the liquid on one gulp.

Maisy gave it a try. It burned awful going down, and she coughed again. Her throat burned.

In a few minutes, she began to feel floaty. The room opened up. She was suspended in a place without walls. Slipping out of the heaviness of her body, she gave herself up to weightlessness and floated in a world without boundaries. The thought of Joey at home alone shot through her mind like a comet, then was quickly gone.

CHAPTER 5

Maizy

The weight of Zane's body tumbled Maizy out of the dreamy cloud in which she'd been floating. She lay under him, a leaden and sweaty heap, the fabric of the couch biting into her back. He was forcing himself into her and the pain was terrible. He grunted and pushed and puffed, and she felt her flesh tear. She felt something hot and wet under her. She hoped it wasn't pee.

"God, you're tight for a fat girl."

Finally he gushed and groaned, then rolled off her. He sat on the edge of the couch and wiped himself with tissues from a box on the table. It was dark now, and the light of the candle he'd lit when they came into the shack filled the room with flickering shadows.

"What time is it?"

Her body ached. She felt raw inside, all the way up to the pit of her stomach.

Between her legs, she felt damp and sticky. She hoped Zane didn't notice the sour, fishy smell she was sure came from the bloody wetness between her legs. She raised her head and looked at her body sprawled there, her shorts and panties tangled around her ankles. She pulled them up, and pulled her shirt down over her bare breasts. Where was her bra? She'd have to find it—didn't want to leave it to be found by some snoopy boy. She pushed her sweaty hair back from her face, feeling fat and dirty. She hoped it was too dark for Zane to see her like that.

It hadn't been how she dreamed it would be, screwed by Zane. Sweet, she'd thought, gentle, him caring that it hurt, asking anxiously, slowing down a little. And then, he'd ask, *Ready? Yes*, she'd say, even if she wasn't, and, with his lips on hers, he'd release his passion, like she'd read in *True Confessions* magazine. They'd lie in each other's arms, maybe doze a little. He wouldn't say he loved her, boys don't like to say it—it embarrasses them. But there'd be a message in his eyes.

She'd built up this scene on each of the nights after he'd rubbed against her in the schoolyard. But it hadn't turned out that way for her.

How had it been for him? Had he hated it? Did she disgust him?

"Time to get going," Zane said. He was zipping up. He looked clean and calm. You couldn't tell he'd just finished screwing a girl. *It's no fair,* she thought. *For him to look so good afterward.*

"Get yourself together. Hell, you bled all over the couch. What'd you do that for?" He was combing his hair, looking in a cracked mirror on the ledge above the couch where the tissues were.

"It was my first time." Her voice shook, came out small, apologizing.

She knew she blushed, like she was telling a dirty joke.

"Don't expect me to believe that, slut. What about all the guys I brought to you?"

"We never done it all the way. I never let no one inside till now."

She felt like crying. Why was he acting like it was her fault they'd done it now, like this, as if she'd even said she would? Not that he'd even given her a chance to say yes or no.

She wanted him to take her in his arms, thank her for what she'd given him. Instead, he'd called her a slut. She wanted to spit out the word like a wad of used-up gum. She felt sick.

"So," he said, his hands jammed in his jeans pockets, standing over her where she still sat on the couch. "Why didn't'cha tell me? What do you expect me to do about it now? Marry you?"

She didn't answer. Took a tissue and wiped her face, under her arms.

"Everyone's gotta have a first time. So you had yours. Come on now, we gotta go."

He blew out the candle and locked the door behind them. Outside, she took deep cutting breaths of the evening air. She wished it was already dark so he couldn't see her.

The shack looked ghostlike in the gray light, a black, scary place where anything could happen. She imagined Zane and his friends sitting around the table at night, in the spooky light of a candle, drinking beer. Would Zane tell the guys about what they'd just done?

She didn't know if she felt sad or angry about what had

34

happened. All she knew was that it couldn't be undone. She was changed forever—and things could never be the same between her and Zane.

What happened in there was important. They were joined together now.

But Maizy was a little put off by Zane. Not mad, she decided, just very disappointed. He acted mean, but she didn't believe it. No. He was just showing off that he'd grown up. He *had* taken her to his secret club and *that* meant something.

"Don't bleed on the seat," he said, opening the car door.

She sat on her sweater, shivering. The first time's never any good. She'd heard that from many girls. If she'd expected it was gonna happen, she'd have been prepared, cleaner, more relaxed. But he'd been so wild for her, he couldn't wait. She liked thinking that. It made up for how he'd forced her, and how he'd acted when it was over. Like it was no big deal. But it *was* important. And they both knew it.

She belonged to Zane now.

CHAPTER 6

Maizy

Maizy got out of Zane's car, forgetting her sweater, and ran the half block home. Her thighs, with the goo and blood congealed, rubbed together as she ran, tearing at her skin. She was sore high up between her legs. She held her flouncing breasts in her hands, uncomfortable without her bra. The street was slick with rain—when had it started to rain, she wondered. And the wind from the lake was clammy. Joey must be scared, home by himself for so long. She hoped he hadn't gone out in the wet street looking for her. He could have been grabbed by the killer.

❖

It looked like every light in her house was lit. She put her key in the lock and opened the front door. Joey was safe, lying on his stomach in front of the radio, as usual.

"Where you been, Maiz?" He twisted around to look at her. "Something happen to you? You don't look so good."

"I'm fine. You okay, Joey? I had a bunch of things to do. Didn't know it'd take so long."

"Pa's home. You're in trouble, Maiz."

Pa came into the room, newspaper in one hand, a beer in the other.

"Where you been?"

His steel blue eyes froze to ice; a white band of anger outlined his mouth. He was a quiet man, one who spoke little and never loud, but his words could slash like a whip. Maizy knew he insisted that his children follow two simple, but unwavering rules. One was they must tell the truth. The other, that Joey never be left alone. They lived, he said, in a dangerous neighborhood. A boy like Joey didn't know good from evil, couldn't take care of himself. It was Maizy's job to watch him when Karl wasn't home.

"The truth," he warned. Over six feet tall, with the hard muscular build of a man who did physical labor, Karl loomed over Maizy with his arms folded on his chest. She felt like a small, fat blob.

Should she tell him she'd been drugged and raped by a boy she'd trusted? No. She wouldn't do that to Zane. The blame was all hers. She'd permitted it, even though she hadn't expected it. In the moment it took her to answer her father's question, she wondered if what had happened in the shack could be called rape. She cleared her throat, trying to find her voice.

"Well? Were you with a boy?"

"Yes."

There. It was out. The way she looked and smelled, he probably could tell anyway. His direct question had made it easier to tell the truth.

The slap slammed her head so far to the side that her

neck creaked. The second slap forced her head to the other side. Her cheeks burned and she sagged, catching herself on the back of a chair.

She heard Joey whimper. She looked for him and saw that he'd gone into the farthest corner of the room and was crouched there, shivering.

She felt blood drip down her chin. She'd bitten her lip. Hot tears stung her cheeks, and her ears rang. She gulped air to keep from screaming, and vomit forced itself between her fingers, even though her hands were clamped over her mouth.

"You slut." His voice hissed with contempt. "You get pregnant, you're out of here, you and your baby."

Pregnant! The icy fear of it struck her like a stab in the heart. But it couldn't be. It never happened the first time. She'd heard that from her girlfriends.

"You stink. Clean yourself up and get Joey's dinner. If it happens again, I'll throw you out. You hear me?"

His voice never rose to a shout, but his words screamed in her ears anyway.

He didn't mean it. She knew that. He had a right to be mad, her leaving Joey alone. But he loved her. He'd never put her out.

In the bathroom, the shower on full strength, she felt rather than heard the front door slam. He'd gone back to work. He'd been on overtime the last few weeks. She swallowed a huge glob of snot and tears.

❖

"Why'd you call him at work?" she asked Joey. She'd belted her robe around her and held two wet towels to her cheeks. "You knew I'd come home soon."

"I didn't call," Joey said. His face was smeared with tears. "He came home early to eat 'cause he had to go back to work. You wasn't here."

"You could've told him I'd be right back. That I just went to the store."

"I didn't know. He went looking for you. Said you wasn't supposed to leave me alone." Joey got up from the floor and went to her. Stretched his short stubby arms around her waist.

"I didn't mean for you to get in trouble, Maiz. Did he hurt you? Do you got a boyfriend now, Maiz? Huh, Maiz?"

"Yeah." She answered both questions.

CHAPTER 7

Zane

"You can get out here," Zane had told Maizy. He'd stopped in the alley behind her house to make sure none of the guys saw her in his car.

He balled up Maizy's damp sweater and threw it in the backseat of the Chevy. People left things behind because they wanted to make sure they'd see you again. Well, forget it. "Bitch," he said aloud. "It'll be a snowy day in August before you see me." He drove slowly down the street.

He had a mix of feelings about what had happened in the shack. Pride was part of it. He'd done it with a girl, first time, and he'd done good. The other guys were always bragging about the girls they'd had. He'd bragged, too, but now he'd know what he was talking about. He felt a little scared, too. What if she blabbed about it and it got back to his dad? Some of the guys' folks went to his dad's church. Well, he'd say she was lying. Who'd ever believe her over him? A fat loser over the minister's son.

Zane checked the time on the car clock. Past six already. He should have been home hours ago, or else called his dad to make up some story about why he'd be late.

40

He was sixteen, for God's sake. Why'd he have to report to his father anymore? What was that about?

He looked down at his crotch for spots. His dad noticed everything.

He opened the window to get rid of the smell of sweat, and Maizy. The air came in cool and smelled of the lake. Fishy. But clean.

He pulled up under a tree on Bryn Mawr, the street before Sheridan, and put the Chevy in neutral. He felt tired, but it was a good tiredness like after a workout. *Sex*, he thought. *And a few smokes*. Like a man feels on his way home after a good day's work.

He slid down and rested his head on the seatback, closed his eyes, and breathed in the evening air.

How could he have known Maizy was cherry? The guys, himself included, feeling her up in the school yard, yet she'd never let them go all the way, though they'd never admitted it to each other. He was *her* first, too. Pleased him somehow—a girl he couldn't stand loved him. Waited for him. Still, if he'd known, maybe he wouldn't've done it. Didn't mean he owed her anything though. And it wasn't all his fault. She could've stopped him.

What made me bring that bitch to the shack? he asked himself. But he knew why. He'd wanted to show off to her—his car, his place, his manhood.

He smiled to himself in the privacy of his car, remembering the day in study hall when she'd caught him staring at her chest. She had remarkable boobs.

"Wanna touch them?" she'd whispered, when the bell rang.

"Sure," he'd said.

It was the first time he'd touched a girl's tits. In a dark space in the schoolyard, where steps led down to a basement door, he'd put his hands in her blouse and under her skirt. He got a hard-on, but she pushed him away. He didn't mind—he didn't want to do it like that, his first time, standing up and in a hurry. After that, she let him feel her up anytime he wanted.

"Wouldja let my buddies have a feel?" he'd asked. "I been telling them how good you are. They're all too scared to ask."

"Do you want me to?" she'd replied, like she was hoping he'd say no.

"Yeah," he said. "It would be a favor to me."

"Okay, then. For you," she said.

The guys appreciated it. Showed them he wasn't just a faggy preacher's son, but a real guy who could get a girl to let him fool around, and let his friends touch her, too.

The guys dug Z's, liked coming to the shack—it gave them a hangout. He was proud when Marko brought the hand of the murdered kid, which he'd found in the garbage the day after she was killed. With the ring still on her finger, just like the paper said. And hairs clutched in the fist. Showed the guys trusted him, considered him one of them. He didn't know why Marko wanted to keep the hand. Why not leave it where he found it, in the trash? But Marko didn't say, and Zane didn't think he should ask. Marko must have his reasons.

Zane had to pee and that broke his trance. When he got back in the car, he started it up and drove slowly down Bryn

Mawr. There were kids all over the place, moms gabbing, fathers coming home from work.

You never saw kids or anyone on Sheridan Road where he lived, except maybe a maid walking a dog. He turned into his street and switched on the radio. Sinatra was singing his latest hit.

❖

His dad knew nothing about Maizy, of course. Or the shack.

"White trash," he called Zane's friends. "Immigrants. Don't ever bring them here. Make friends in your own neighborhood, where you belong."

Zane hated the kids who went to his dad's church. They only went because their folks made them, and they probably hated it as much as he did. Jerks. They snubbed him for not having the grades to be accepted to the stupid private school, and for not being in the church band. Not that he cared. Bunch of prissy slobs. But none of them had a car, though. Well, the hell with them.

He drove slowly, taking his time, in no big hurry to get home.

❖

Getting the Chevy on his sixteenth birthday had been the surprise of his life. It wasn't new, but it was in good condition, white, with black leather upholstery. Not really a sharp car, not what he'd have chosen, but still, it was his own car. He'd have hugged his dad when he handed him the keys, but there was no hugging between them, ever, and hardly any touching at all. Still, he'd reached out for his father's hand and shook it in thanks.

But there'd been rules that went with the car. He couldn't drive at night, couldn't take more than one passenger at a time. No girls allowed, and he was to stay away from those loser kids and hillbillies on Kenmore. And no joy riding!

He wasn't supposed to drive on Kenmore at all, but shit! He'd been to the shack nearly every day. Most of the other guys never came, had summer jobs. But Fred Fink didn't have a job, couldn't get one so far. He'd be there with his art stuff and they'd work on cartoons. Fred was really good, and he was teaching Zane a lot. And they'd take long drives in the Chevy—downtown to a movie at the Chicago Theater. Or they'd go to Lincoln Park and just hang, watching girls and eating sandwiches or hot dogs.

He had to be careful though, make sure he didn't get caught. Because guys who knew his dad from church said they'd seen the Rev walking on Kenmore—like he was looking for someone. And they'd seen him in the park, too. They'd seen him near the basketball hoop, next to the men's and ladies' toilets, watching them toss balls.

Probably looking for me, Zane thought. *Trying to catch me breaking the rules about the car.*

❖

No way did he feel like going home. He wanted to keep driving all the way to Evanston. It'd be cool to park the car, near the cemetery where Chicago ends and Evanston begins. He'd walk to the beach, maybe pick up a North Side girl and go to Ned's for a Coke.

Without thinking about it, Zane passed his driveway and kept driving north. Pulled into a Walgreen's parking lot and called home from a phone booth. If his father answered, he'd make an excuse for being late, then just turn around and head home.

Miss Verner answered the phone on the first ring.

"You missed dinner," she said. "The Reverend went to a meeting. I'm leaving now. Your dinner's in the oven."

All right! Nobody home. He'd drive to Evanston, park on Orrington, and get a pizza. And he'd order a beer.

Maybe he'd walk along the lake all the way to the Northwestern campus.

Evanston was the best city in the world, a clean town full of college kids. Sharp-looking girls. He could try to get one of them in the car and drive to the city limits, find a motel. Nah. He knew that wouldn't work. They liked jocks, and he was just a dumb high school kid—and looked it. He stretched up to look at himself in the rearview mirror. Skin oily, a new zit starting on his chin. Only girl would want him was a fat slut like Maizy.

He found a parking space, turned off the motor, leaned back on the seat, and let the breeze blow through the car. A Guy Lombardo song was on the radio . . . mushy stuff.

Across the street was Evanston Hospital, where his mom died.

CHAPTER 8

Zane

He'd been four when his mom died, so he didn't have a lot of memories. The last time he saw her was in a room in the hospital. Evanston Hospital. Her eyes were closed, and her face was white and blank.

"Kiss your mama goodbye," the nurse said. But he didn't want to and ran out of the room.

They never talked about her, him and his dad.

She must have held him when he was little, hugged him. He thought she probably loved him like other moms loved their babies. He couldn't remember. She was dead twelve years, but he never thought of it in years. It just seemed like forever.

❖

Tonight the hospital was lit up, sick people behind the windows, having supper. Hospital food probably tasted bad, like Miss Verner's cooking.

He wasn't hungry. He got out of the car, walked east toward Lake Michigan. Flying ghosts of lightning skimmed the sky. The street was full of shadows. He felt drawn to the lake.

He knew that a mother would be on your back all the time to do stuff that was good for you. Scold you for cussing, but wouldn't laugh at you for wanting a light in your room at night. You could cry in front of her and not be ashamed.

Had he loved his mom? Zane couldn't remember ever loving anyone.

The wind was getting stronger, shaking loose some leaves that should have had more time on the trees. Things ended too soon: summer vacation, daylight, the good feeling of making out with a girl, a mother dying when her kid was young.

Fred Fink's mom was okay. She liked having kids around. Didn't ask stupid questions, gave out milk and homemade cookies. Didn't mind hearing their music. She was no pin-up, just a middle-aged lady with a lumpy body, her hair getting gray. But he liked her, a lot. It was a real home when you had a mom in it.

He and his dad were just two guys living in the same house, like roommates. His friends asked him, "What's it like with a minister for a father? Do you have to pray a lot? Read the Bible? Does he talk about God and heaven and hell?"

That shit? Not at Zane's house. They hardly ever talked about anything. He wondered if his dad even liked him at all.

❖

By now, the lake was black, with silver-tipped waves coming in fast and wild, crashing against the rocks—like it wanted to escape its prison and flood the world. Zane wondered: What happens to a body part thrown in the lake? Is it swept out to another shore, ending up on a faraway beach, or does it stay close, tossed about by the waves and tides, and finally wash up near where it was thrown in the first place?

What if someone forgot to lock the shack and a stray dog got into the shack and dug up the hand? It could end up being traced back to them, and then they'd be in deep shit.

It started to rain. Big cold drops, like the giant's tears in Fred's cartoons. Zane started back to Orrington, where he'd parked the car.

❖

Except for getting the Chevy, so far it had been a bad summer. When school started in September, he'd be a senior and start applying to college. His dad wanted him to go to the seminary. Study for the ministry.

Sucks, Zane thought. He wanted to go to the Chicago Art Institute. He was going to be a cartoonist. But he'd never get his dad to put out for art school. To the Rev, artists were drunks and drifters.

Fred Fink was going to Illinois State University, and it didn't cost hardly anything. But Zane's father hated state schools. Playgrounds, he called them.

❖

The rain splashed in cold, heavy drops, turning the pavement into a blur of colors, reflecting the neon lights of the shops. It was beautiful. Someday he'd paint a picture of a night street in the rain.

He got in the car, soaked. He grabbed Maizy's sweater from the backseat, dried himself off, and started for home. He switched on the radio: Cole Porter's "Anything Goes."

❖

He walked through the huge dark house to the kitchen. He didn't bother to heat the plate of food Miss Verner had left, ate cold roast beef and mashed potatoes, a dried-out biscuit, and threw the beans in the garbage. Drank some milk in gulps from the carton, washing down two sugar donuts.

In his bedroom, he peeled off his wet clothes, and stuffed them in the hamper.

He liked to sleep in the raw, but he pulled on pajamas, sure his dad would look in on him when he got home. Sleeping naked was a sin, according to his dad, and led to dirty dreams.

He gathered the quilt against him, and in the half world before sleep, felt himself grow hard thinking of Maizy's body under him, her arms around him.

CHAPTER 9

Fred

When the guys got together at Z's, which wasn't that often except for Zane and me—I guess they had better things to do than meet in that old shack—we mostly talked about the hand they'd buried under the floor slat. Chip wanted to turn it over to the cops and get a reward. I thought it was crazy to hold out evidence they maybe could use to find the pervert who'd killed the little kid.

But Marko said it was too late for a reward, and besides, we'd be in trouble for keeping it so long. Besides which, he was already in trouble with the cops, and having a hand they were looking for wasn't going to help him any. He said he'd kill anyone who ratted to the cops. Zane agreed we should keep it and shut up about it. He thought it was cool to have something so gruesome buried in the floor.

"Want to see it?" he asked me.

"No way," I said. It would make me sick.

I wondered when it would begin to stink.

❖

Mostly, I was at the shack alone. I brought my inks and sketchpad, and I worked on my comic strips. I've got this hero figure, a young guy who can morph into any kind of creature. He can sting the evil guys, or poison their guts. He can turn into an eagle and grab the villain in his talons, and drop him into a volcano or on an iceberg to freeze to death. He can fly, too, to rescue victims on wings like angels, and pluck them out of fires or car wrecks or wars.

I've been doing this comic strip for a long time.

Sometimes Zane showed up at the shack in his Chevy, and we'd take off for the beach or downtown to see a movie.

I like Zane a lot. He was my first friend here. He's different from the others—the tough guys, the dropouts. They don't really go for us either. They just tolerate Zane, who's always playing up to them, trying to be like them, talking their talk, which isn't him at all. Jeez, he's got his own wheels, plenty of dough, better duds than any of us, but it's like he's gotta prove he's as good as them, when really, he's whole a lot better.

We could be good friends. He's going to college like me. No way is he going to hang out on the street, get in trouble with the cops. He's not that kind of guy, even if he pretends he is.

He likes my comic strips, wants me to teach him how to draw cartoons. He's got good ideas for action figures. Maybe someday we'll do a strip together and sell it to a syndicate, make a lot of dough, even become famous.

Maizy's nuts about him. You can tell by how her face lights up when I mention his name. She'd do anything for him. So why does he put her down all the time? I don't get it.

One scorching day, he picks me up at the shack, where I'm inking in a new sketch, to go for a drive.

"Does the car stink?" he asks.

"Not at all," I say. "Leather could use a polish. Want me to do it for you?"

"Nah," he says. "You sure it doesn't smell of sex?"

I know he's going to brag about having sex in the car. He likes to blab how he makes it with college girls he says he picks up in Evanston.

"Nope," I say. "No smell."

"You ever do it with a virgin?" Now he's going to tell me he did. In the car.

"Maybe," I say. I'm not about to tell him I never did it with anyone. I push up the volume of the radio. I don't want to deal with this or hear about it.

"Would you believe Maizy was cherry?"

He turns his head to look at me, to see if I'm impressed. I don't answer. I don't know if I should believe he did it with Maizy. This whole conversation makes me want to puke.

A car honks. He's in the wrong lane.

"Watch where you're going," I tell him.

"Would you believe it, Maizy never had anyone before me?"

He expects me to pat him on the back, tell him how great he is, that he did it with a girl who'd do anything for him because she goes for him big-time. I didn't know if she was a virgin or not. I never asked.

"Did you force her?" Soon's I ask, I know I shouldn't have.

"What? You think I'd have to?" His voice is ice cold now. I've insulted him.

"Nah," he says, getting over his burn in a minute. "She wanted it, bad. You gonna ask me if the slut is a good lay?"

"No. I'm not gonna ask," I say. I hate this whole conversation. I don't know if I'm mad because he did it with her, or because of the way he's talking about her.

"Know something?" I say. "I just remembered I got a dentist appointment. I got to go home."

He gets it. I burned him again. "Then you're going to have to take the bus," he says. "I'm not going back to Kenmore today. My dad don't want me going there."

He stops the car. We're at Belmont, at least five miles from Kenmore.

"Lend me bus fare?" I ask. "I'm flat."

"Sorry. I got no money on me."

It's ninety degrees out. A long walk home.

I get out and kick the back tire as he takes off.

CHAPTER 10

Fred

I was out of the Chevy before Zane came to a full stop, swearing I'd never get in that car again.

Screw Zane. It was broiling hot, with enough humidity to make you feel like you're in a steam room. A typical summer day in Chicago. I crossed Sheridan Road, and what seemed like miles of grass strewn with bodies toasting in the sun, and hiked to the lakefront.

It was no cooler. The rocky breakwater shimmered with heat waves and the water glared like the sun caught in a mirror. I stripped off my shirt and stuck it in the pocket of my shorts. Took a massive drink from the water fountain and started walking on the rocks. Not many people around there, just more fool bodies spread out like slabs of steak, barbecuing themselves.

My brain was boiling, but I had to figure out what happened, from when Zane picked me up at Z's, to when he dumped me miles from home, and no dough for carfare. Why was he so pissed?

He must've got the feeling I was pissed by him screwing Maizy. Or that I was putting him down when I asked if he forced her. What kind of guy blabs about doing a girl, and then calls her a slut for liking him so much that she'd let him do it?

Maybe something I said—or the way I said it—made him think I liked her. That I was jealous of him, and it made him sore. That's crazy. If he wanted her for his girl, it was okay with me. I sure didn't want her. I just didn't like him putting her down.

It was none of my business. Nothing to me, so why didn't I just listen to him blab, act like I was impressed, which is what he'd expected. It's dumb to get on the wrong side of your only friend. He'd probably spread a lot of crap about me. Say I'm a fag. Or that I'm sweet on Maizy, his girl. Can't ever tell what someone like Zane will do if you piss him off. I guess I didn't dig the guy like I thought I did. Thought he was smarter than the others, his dad being a reverend and all.

Was Maizy really cherry, like Zane said? I believed it. She let guys make out with her, but she probably stopped them before going all the way, like she told Zane.

Did he actually force her, or was she so crazy about him that she'd let him do it? Did she *want* him to, like he said? What I think is, he must've forced her. Maybe she tried to fight him off. Probably why he got so mad when I asked. He didn't take it like I meant it. As half joking, half serious. Could he have actually raped Maizy? That wouldn't sit well with me.

Did I accuse him of forcing her because I wanted it to be that, rather than her letting him, or actually wanting it, like he'd claimed? I tried not to get too worked up about the whole thing. It was too hot, and I had a long way to walk.

❖

I'm beat when I get to Kenmore—the walk took over an hour. I want a Coke in the grocery store where it's cooler. But I have no money on me, so I just have to hoof it home and drink a gallon of ice water. I have to pass Maizy's house on the way. I hope she won't be sitting on the step like she usually does around this time of day, watching Joey. I don't really feel like talking to her right now, after all that stuff with Zane and his bragging.

"Hey, Fred Fink."

Shit. She's in front of her house, standing by the gushing fire hydrant with Joey. They have their shoes off, letting the water splash on their legs. Maizy's braid is loose, with her lemon-colored hair down her neck and around her face. She's wearing coveralls, with a sleeveless shirt underneath. Her face has bruises on it, like she's been hit. I bet that slime Zane must've bashed her.

"Hey," I say. I stoop to get a handful of water from the hydrant and gulp it down.

"You look like you been running a race," she says. "Wait here with Joey and I'll get you an ice-cold drink. Orange okay?"

"Yeah," I say.

"Joey, say hello to Fred Fink," she says before going in the house, pushing Joey in front of me.

" 'Lo," Joey says, and gives me a big wet smile, his tongue hanging outta his mouth like a thirsty dog.

Joey don't look right to me. He's supposed to be eight, but he looks like he's about six. Got slit eyes and short, bulky arms. Fat face, but a scrawny body. His legs that he's got in the water are stubby, too. His face is scrunched together, and his hair's so thin it don't hardly cover his scalp. Still, he's a happy little kid, splashing around in the cold water, stamping his feet, laughing like he's hearing a comedy on the radio.

Maybe he's backward.

"What happened to your face?" I ask Maizy when she brings out drinks in sweating bottles.

Her face turns red under the bruises.

"Nothin'." She finger-combs her hair down over her face to hide the marks.

"Our pa whopped her," Joey says, reaching for one of the bottles.

So it wasn't Zane.

"What for?" I ask. I know she doesn't want to talk about it, but I'm mad at everyone now, and I don't care who I hurt anymore.

"Shut up, Joey," she says. "Family thing," she tells me. "It's fine now, though. So forget about it, okay?"

I take a bottle and gulp the drink, saying nothing.

"Thanks." I give her back the bottle. "I gotta go now."

I'm sweaty and itchy, and I feel like I walked a million miles uphill in the desert. I'm in no mood to gab with Maizy. Or to feel sorry right now that she has a pa who hits her.

CHAPTER 11

Maizy

Maizy returned to the open hydrant where Joey was sucking his drink from the bottle and prancing joyously in the splashing water.

"Having fun, Joey?" she asked her brother.

"Yeah, man, Maiz!" He'd picked that up from the other kids, *yeah, man.* "Can I get my head wet?"

"Sure. But give me the bottle. I'll keep it for later."

Joey lay down on the wet cement, letting the water douse the front of his small square body, his arms flapping like a bird.

Two kids playing stickball down the street must of heard Joey's happy screams and walked over. *Don't make trouble,* Maizy prayed.

"Hey, Joey, who says you can use up all the water?" In seconds, their shoes were off and their jeans were rolled up.

"Move over." The taller boy pushed Joey out of the stream.

"Maizy!" Joey got to his feet, his face tragic.

"We can all share," Maizy said. "There's plenty water."

But now the water felt cold on her legs. The fun had gone out of it. She went to the step and dried herself with the towel she'd brought out for Joey. The edges of her shorts were wet and felt clammy against her thighs. The bruise on her face burned where the sun hit it.

She hadn't wanted Fred to know her pa hit her. It would give him the wrong idea about her family. She wanted Fred to think good of her. Maizy didn't know why it mattered so much what Fred thought. It just did. He'd think Pa hit her because she did something bad, or else maybe that Pa was a drunk, or cruel. *I don't want him to think neither of those things,* she told herself. *Neither one's true.*

She sat on the step, the towel over her head against the hot sun, watching the boys play in the water. Joey shouldn't've told Fred that Pa hit her. But Joey didn't know any better. You always had to tell him what to say. Or not say. He'd never mean to embarrass her in front of Fred. It wouldn't occur to him.

What happened at the shack didn't mean she'd done something bad. Zane had surprised her, wanting her so much he couldn't help himself. Maybe if he knew she was a virgin, he wouldn't have done it all the way, just fooled around instead. Maybe if she'd tried to stop him, it wouldn't have happened the way it did. But she hadn't tried. Now they'd done it, and if you loved each other, doing it had to be okay. It was just a way of loving, wasn't it?

Her ma had told her that everything you did depended on your intentions. If your intention was good, what happened wasn't wrong. Her ma would understand why she went all the way with Zane. Maizy missed her ma. A girl really needed a ma, especially when she was trying to grow up, like now.

But Pa wasn't a cruel man and he never got drunk. He tried to take good care of her and Joey. He'd hit her because he didn't understand what had happened. He didn't *intend* to hurt her, but to teach her. She hadn't *intended* to leave Joey alone, either, to be with Zane. It's just the way it ended up.

Maizy didn't know what was going to happen next between her and Zane.

I'll try and explain it all to Fred next time I see him, she thought. She could tell Fred anything. She didn't know if she'd tell him the whole thing, though. Some things between lovers should be private. But she didn't want him to think bad of her. Fred was a good friend. She didn't want to lose him.

"Joey," she called, "time to go inside. I have to start making supper."

"Please, Maiz. I don't wanna go inside. Please, Maiz?" Joey thought he could do anything he wanted if he said please. It was something she'd taught him, and it had made him spoiled, always getting his way.

"You can listen to the cowboy show on the radio. It's about to start now."

She couldn't take a chance leaving him outside alone. If one of the boys decided to hit him or he fell and hurt himself, Pa would really be mad.

❖

It was nearly a week since Pa'd slapped her, and he'd been real nice after that, like he was sorry he'd done it. He wouldn't say so though; it just wasn't his way.

She started gathering stuff together to fix their supper. She'd make tomato soup from the Campbell's can, a salad, and some rice, easy food to eat, because they'd all had stomachaches after last night's supper. Maybe the hamburger meat was too old, or the spinach'd gone sour. They'd had to take turns for the bathroom. She thought Pa would holler at her for trying to poison them, but all he'd said was maybe they'd got a bug.

Pa and Joey were all right in the morning, but Maizy still felt sick. She'd felt bad yesterday, too, before eating the hamburger. And come to think of it, the day before, too.

Guess I got a bug and the others caught it, and it wasn't even the food, she thought. *I won't eat nothing else, only the soup tonight.*

August is the hottest month in Chicago. Sometimes there's a little breeze from the lake, but mostly the heat sits on you like an electric blanket that you can't turn off. Maizy had sat on her step every day since being with Zane, not even going to the grocery store to shop, or the laundry, for fear she'd miss him when he came to see her. She was sure he'd be coming down Kenmore in his car someday to take her for a ride. Maybe he'd want them to do it again, and she would. She might even like it, next time. Another reason she was sure he'd come by was she'd left her bra at the shack. When Zane found it, he'd want to return it.

She'd been fixing herself up more. She went inside several times to wet her hair and wash the sweat off her face. She wore her longest shorts to hide the fat on her thighs, and put on clean white shirts. She noticed the clothes fit looser. Maybe she was getting thinner. She still felt sick from the bug. Mornings she couldn't even look at food, and she sometimes threw up after fixing breakfast.

She should go over to the clinic and get some pills for her upset stomach. She must have a bad bug. She felt nauseated all the time, especially in the morning. Her period was late, but that wasn't unusual for her. The doctor at the clinic had told her she'd regulate if she got thinner. It was worth feeling sick if it made her get thin. Zane would like her better.

Maizy hadn't seen Fred Fink either, since that day the hydrant was open. She missed talking to him, but she didn't want him sitting on her step if Zane came by. Didn't take much to make a guy jealous.

It got to be September, but still hot, and stickier than ever. But Zane still hadn't come, and now school had started. He'd be a senior now, but it didn't matter because Maizy wasn't going back to school anymore.

"You got held back," Pa said, "so it's just as well you stop going. I never went past fifth grade. You'll be like a ma now, taking care of Joey and cleaning the house."

"I still done all that and went to school," she'd told Pa.

"Now you'll do it better," Pa said. "Maybe not sitting

on your ass at a school desk all day, you'll lose some of that weight."

But he was wrong about that. She'd finally got over the bug, and now it seemed like she was always hungry. And she'd gained back all the weight she'd lost.

She didn't want to quit school. Not only because of Zane, but she had girlfriends there and she liked that, liked how they gossiped about boys and complained about teachers. Not going to school made her feel grown-up too soon. She wasn't through being a kid yet.

With everyone else back at school, it was quiet on the street. The only people around were young moms pushing strollers or tugging little kids, and old ladies in aprons sitting on their steps, their white, veiny legs stretched out to get the sun.

She never saw the man from the park lavatory anymore. She wondered what would have happened if she'd told the cops about seeing him in the lav with the little girl. Would they have believed her and gone after him?

Had he been the one who killed Marta? No one knew yet who did it. Seemed like the police'd stopped looking. The whole thing was like a dream now, except for Marta being dead. When she saw the moms with their little kids, she thought of Marta. Did Anna still go to the park and watch the children play?

I'll take Joey to the park after school one day, she thought. *Maybe I'll see Anna and we can talk.*

❖

After walking Joey to school most mornings, Maizy cleaned the house, doing the corners and drawers, and even above the windows. She shopped at the A & P now because it was cheaper than the grocery. Maizy had more time, now that she didn't go to school. She even got a cookbook out of the library so she could learn to make different things than hamburgers, baked potatoes, and canned vegetables.

The allowance Pa gave her for food went further at the A & P, and she often had money left over. With it, she bought a lipstick and a fancy hairbrush, feeling guilty buying something for herself from the food money.

I should save it up in case Pa loses his job, she thought. *Or I could buy something for Joey, roller skates, so he could be more like other kids.*

Evenings, after Joey was in bed and Pa was reading his paper, or out with his pals, Maizy sat out on the step. She watched gown-ups and kids having fun, girls walking by with their boyfriends, arm-in-arm or smooching right on the street, right in front of everyone.

Maizy felt lonely and left out. She missed Zane. She thought about him all day, every day. She went over every minute of their time together. The thought of his hands on her made her crazy with wanting him. When she thought of his fingers touching her, her panties got wet. At night, in bed, she touched herself and got relief, but it was a sin. She knew that. She shouldn't, but she couldn't help it. She wanted him and ached for him.

Did Zane go to the shack after school? She knew he had to be careful to stay away from Kenmore, in case his pa came looking for him. Did he find her bra? Maybe he never found it. It could've got pushed under the couch and no-body ever saw it. Boys didn't look under things. Or maybe he kept it. She liked to think of him sleeping with it on his pillow, smelling her body on it. He wanted her as much as she wanted him. She just knew it.

She thought of gong to Z's some morning, when no one would be there. She'd look around for the bra. She'd take a plate of fresh-baked cookies for the guys to find when they came after school. Zane would know she brought it. And he'd brag that his girl was a good cook.

CHAPTER 12

Zane

Zane heard footsteps approaching his room in time to switch off the radio and grab a *National Geographic* before his father walked in. Without knocking, as usual.

"Yes, Dad?" In his mind, he added, *What in hell do you want? When will I ever get some privacy!*

"If you have any plans for this weekend, there's plenty of time to cancel them."

His father picked a sock and a pair of underwear off the floor. "Did you forget where the laundry hamper is?"

"I do happen to have plans, Dad. Why do I have to cancel them?"

He didn't have anything special, but he wanted to be with the guys. Especially Fred Fink. He hadn't spoken to Fred since the day he'd kicked him out of the car, but he didn't want to be on the outs with him. He liked the guy. Fred had more smarts than any of the others, even Marko, and he was going to teach him how to do those spiffy cartoons he was always drawing.

Zane liked to draw. He was good at it. He wanted to take a class at the Art Institute next summer vacation. He did caricatures, especially of biblical figures. His dad had found the one of St. Francis, a hawk sitting on his nose. He'd been furious. Sacrilege, he'd called it, and tore it up. One of his best, Zane thought. He'd been mad at his dad. What right did he have . . . ?

"We're going on a retreat," his dad said. "We leave Friday. Be back Sunday. We'll be worshipping at the Church of the Dells."

"A retreat? Why do I have to go? I hate retreats. Just old guys sitting around and praying. Kids don't go on re-treats."

"This is a retreat for fathers and sons," his dad said. "There'll be hiking and fishing. Barbecues. Swimming in the river."

"I can't go, Dad. I've got a game Saturday afternoon. And gobs of homework."

"I talked to Jerome Williams at the church meeting last night. He'll arrange with the coach to let you off for Sat-urday's game. We leave Friday after school."

Mr. Williams was principal of Kenmore Senior High and, just Zane's luck, a member of the church. So it was al-ready settled. Damn.

"Pack warm clothes. It gets cold at night. Now why don't you put that magazine away and do some of the homework you were planning for this weekend? It's Tues-day. You have plenty of time to get it done before we go."

Zane sighed. Another weekend shot to hell. But then he had a brainstorm. What if Fred went along?

"Can we take one of my friends? He hasn't got a fa-ther. It would be a good deed."

Fred would go for it. Probably never been to the Dells, or anywhere for that matter, being a kid from a poor family. They could sneak off on their own and have a ball, even drink. His dad would have everybody on a program, so they'd never even be missed.

"One of those immigrants from Kenmore? Absolutely not. Now if you had a decent friend—"

"He's not an immigrant, Dad. He was born in Chicago. They moved to Kenmore this summer, after his dad died. He's real smart—going to college when he graduates. Please, Dad."

"Well, tell him to come to dinner this week. Then we'll see."

Absolutely not done, Zane thought. *You don't ask guys to dinner.*

But his father had already left the room. Why couldn't he ever close the door?

❖

"Fred, wait up," Zane called. Fred was on his way to chemistry, threading his way through the kids loitering in the hall. Fred always had to be early, like a real jerk.

"Yeah?" Fred had been giving him the deep freeze, ever since the car thing. "What d'you want?"

"I gotta talk to you about something."

He'd play it cool, like nothing had happened between them.

❖

68

"Look," Zane said when they got together on the steps after school, "I'm sorry about—"

"It's okay," Fred interrupted. "No sweat. So what d'you want?"

"Ever been to the Dells?"

"Nope. Never been anywhere. What's the Dells?"

"It's in Wisconsin, an Indian reservation. Sort of a vacation place. With campgrounds, and a lodge. It's got rock formations. Cliffs, and a real good river for canoeing and swimming. My dad's taking me there for the weekend. He says you can come with us."

"Yeah? Well, I don't know. I can ask my ma. She likes me to be around on weekends. When's it going to be?"

"This weekend. Come to my house for dinner and my dad will clue us in."

He wasn't going to mention that it was a retreat and scare Fred off.

"I'll ask Ma when she gets home. Call me tonight, I'll let you know."

"Fred's coming to eat with us tomorrow night, like you said," Zane told his dad at dinner. "Is that okay?"

They'd said grace and eaten potpies. No conversation, as usual. They were on dessert, canned peaches and graham crackers, Miss Verner's specialty.

"Tell Miss Verner he's coming. He's to be on time and wearing clean clothes."

"I told him about the retreat. He has to ask his mom."

"Hmm. Well, I hope you didn't promise him anything before I meet him."

"I didn't promise him anything. Just *told* him about it. He probably won't even want to go."

Jeez, Zane thought, *the guy has to pass inspection like he was getting to see the president, just to go on a lousy retreat.* What a dope his dad was.

❖

He asked Miss Verner if she'd please make some kind of meat for dinner, not tuna fish casserole. She almost never made real food.

"Could you make a pie? My friend doesn't get much chance to eat pie."

"He'd better have good manners." Miss Verner sniffed. "Your dad doesn't like messy eating."

❖

Fred came home with Zane after school. His ma had made him wear his dress-up clothes to school for going to the minister's house.

"She said it was an honor to be asked, and that I had to dress up," Fred said.

Some honor, Zane thought. And he probably got better food at home.

❖

"Dad, this is my friend, Fred Fink. Fred, my dad, Dr. Caruthers."

They'd been playing a checkers game in Zane's room, but at exactly six, they'd appeared in the dining room. The Reverend was already seated.

"Fink? Is that a German name?"

"I don't know, sir. My ma said it was shortened."

They said grace, heads bowed. Zane watched Fred out of the corner of his eye. Probably never said grace before, but at least the guy knew what to do.

"Zane tells me you're going to college when you graduate," the minister said.

"Yes, sir. Illinois State."

"That's a play school. You going to join one of those fraternities and do a lot of drinking? Is that why you're going to Illinois?"

"No, sir. I'm going there because it's a state school, and it's all my ma can afford. I couldn't join a fraternity. Costs too much money. And I won't be drinking."

Wow, Zane thought. *He's no fool. All the right answers.*

❖

Later, when Fred had left to walk home across Sheridan Road, Zane confronted his father. He was in his study, going through a pile of pictures. Covered them up when Zane came in. As if he would even want to see anything his father was working on.

"Was Fred okay, Dad? Can he come?"

"He's a good boy, Zane. Good manners. Respectful. Jewish, isn't he? Fink, for Finkelstein."

71

Zane had never thought of Fred's religion. What did that matter anyway? As long as he wasn't a member of his dad's church.

"Well, he's not an immigrant. So, can I ask him?"

"We'll be having church services. Tell him that. Some Jews are against hearing the Lord's word."

Zane knew he wouldn't say anything about church or services.

❖

The orange buses pulled up at five thirty. Zane grabbed the box suppers and two sleeping bags, an extra one for Fred. Fred was excited about the trip. He didn't know about the church part, but it was too late to back out now.

"We're on the first bus," Zane said. "We're supposed to sit up front."

He and Fred put their stuff on the shelf over their seats and sat behind the driver. His dad had a special seat at the front of the bus, facing the passengers. By six, everyone was aboard and the driver put the bus in gear.

"Who are these guys, Zane? Are we the only kids?" Fred twisted around in his seat and gawked at the busload of adults.

"My dad said it's a father and son thing," Zane said. "The rest of the kids are probably on the next bus."

"These old geezers have kids?" Fred asked.

The bus lumbered out of the driveway onto Sheridan Road, eased its way into the rush-hour traffic.

"Welcome, members," Reverend Caruthers said to the passengers on the bus using a megaphone. He wore a tan business suit and a visor cap with United Church of God, the name of the church, across its front, in white letters. "We're on our way to worship God in one of nature's wonderlands."

Why can't he dress casual, like everyone else? Zane groaned inwardly.

The passengers murmured their response. *A bunch of old church prigs,* Zane thought, *dressed in their ideas of camping duds.* They wore Sears Roebuck casual clothes, mostly in dark colors. The racks above the seats were stuffed with their gear.

Fred poked him. "Worship God?" he whispered.

"Just his way of talking," Zane answered.

"We've got a long ride ahead," his father announced. "I trust you all brought box suppers. Eat when you're hungry. Sleep if you're so inclined. But no snoring!"

A burst of laughter from the group.

"We'll make rest stops every two hours. Don't disturb your neighbors with loud talk unless you're talking to God. Then sing out loud and clear." He smiled, showing large teeth. "Thank you, God, for sending us on this retreat in Your honor, this chance to get away from our daily toil and commune with You through the beauties of nature." The Reverend Caruthers spread his arms and turned his head upward, as if he could see the sky through the roof of the bus.

"Amen," the passengers answered.

Damn, Zane thought. Churching started already. He

glanced at Fred to see how he was taking it. Fred had joined in the *amens*.

"Now all together in praise of our Lord. Let's sing 'Down by the River.'" The Reverend blew a note on a pitch pipe and the busload sang with zest.

Zane glanced again at Fred. What was he thinking of all this? Probably wondering what he'd gotten himself into.

"Zane." His dad, raising his hand, stopped the singing.

Shit, Zane thought. What had he done? Why did they have to sit in front, right under his father's eye?

"Aren't you and your friend going to raise your voices to the Lord?"

"Fred doesn't know the words, Dad."

His dad turned to Fred, his smile shrunk to a pucker.

"Or is it because you're Jewish?"

Zane could feel everyone on the bus listening. He could feel Fred's confusion.

It was going to be a long bus ride.

CHAPTER 13

Fred

It had gotten very quiet on the bus. Everyone was listening to the Rev and me. I looked at Zane to get a hint of what to say to the Rev about being Jewish. Zane was staring out the window; no help there. I thought of saying, "No, it's not because of my being some part Jewish that I didn't do the sing-along. It's because I think it's stupid. Why would you be singing God songs on a bus going on a camping trip?" But I remembered my manners.

"I'm a quarter Jewish by birth, sir," I said. "My pa was half Jewish. But he's dead. Ma's Unitarian. But we don't go to church."

"She against religion?" he asked.

I didn't know what he was getting at. Did you have to sing Bible songs to go to the Dells? Or belong to a religion? Zane hadn't said. What had I gone and got myself in for?

"No, sir. I think she wants me to choose my own religion when I grow up," I said, thinking it was as good an answer as any, and true, too.

"Well," the Rev said, "maybe after this retreat, you'll

join our church." Everyone said "amen." I looked at Zane. His face was red as a tomato.

I didn't say anything, but I made up my mind that if I ever joined a church, it sure wouldn't be his. He started another song—something about walking in the fields of the Lord. Zane poked me and I did like he was—I moved my mouth like I was singing. Zane actually knew the words.

When Zane asked me if I wanted to go camping at the Dells, I was surprised. I thought he was still pissed at me for insinuating he forced Maizy, and *I* was sure burned at *him,* kicking me out of his car miles from home on a scorching hot day. But he wanted to get back to being friends, and I sure didn't want to be on the outs with Zane, him being my best friend and all, and the only friend I got at school. And a camping trip sounded good to me, something a kid does with a father. I didn't know it was going to be a church deal. Zane shoulda told me.

❖

After the singing, the minister said we should eat. Good. I was starved. Ma wanted to send along some fried chicken for Zane and me, and some chocolate cupcakes she made, but he said never mind, Miss Verner was putting up box suppers.

It was starting to get dark and the lights in the bus went on. Zane took out sandwiches wrapped in foil—peanut butter and jelly, which I like, but not for supper. One for each of us. I coulda eaten three. And graham crackers like we had at his house. Maybe graham crackers is a church thing, but cupcakes are a lot better. Plain old water to drink, no Cokes. At least it was cold. Miss Verner isn't much of a good cook. I could smell other people's food, roast beef sandwiches, even fried chicken, pickles, chips. I couldn't see what the minister was eating. Not peanut butter, I bet.

We pulled into a rest stop out in the country and everyone got off to pee. There was a vending machine in the men's, and I bought Oh Henrys for Zane and me to eat later on.

Back on the bus again, the minister had everyone say a prayer, which I didn't mouth because the bus lights were dim and it was too dark for him to see my lips. Then he walked down the aisle, saying "good night" and "God bless you" to all the passengers.

"No talking, go to sleep," he warned Zane and me. We weren't talking, and it was too early to go to sleep, but the dark and the moving of the bus made me drowsy. Zane dozed off first.

I put my seat back and started to think about Maizy. Last time I saw her was the day Zane kicked me out of his car. She didn't want me to know her pa hit her, but Joey told me. Did her pa know about her doing it with Zane, and that's why he hit her? Or was it for something else? Maybe Zane was lying and they didn't do it at all. Whatever. Her pa shouldn't have hit her though.

I thought of the day I first met Maizy and we made out in her basement—how soft her body was, and how nice she was to me. I liked Maizy as a friend, but not the same as guys like girls. I never did go for a girl that way; never will, I guess.

Why'd she have to let all the guys feel her up? She said she didn't mind, but I think she did it to please Zane. She liked him a lot.

I poked Zane to see if he was awake.

"Yeah?" he whispered.

"Is something wrong with Joey?"

"Maizy's bro? Yeah. Retarded. "

"Did you and her really do it?"

"Maizy? Yeah."

"Did she want to?"

"Sorta. I didn't know it was her first time. What's it to you anyway? You like her?"

" 'Course not."

"You want to do it with her? You could, you know. I can fix it."

"No," I say. "Don't be fixing it with guys. It's not fair."

"Why not? If she's willing?"

"She likes you, Zane. A lot."

"You're crazy. I know her all my life almost." He didn't say anything for a while. "I gotta stay away from her. If my father ever found out . . ."

"Who's gonna tell him? I'm not. She'd never tell him."

"What if I knocked her up?"

"Could you have?"

"Don't know. Doubt it, first time and all."

"What if you did? What would you do?"

"Nothing. No one'd believe it was me."

"You'd say it wasn't?"

"Hell, yes, if she claimed it was. Everyone knows she's a slut."

I hated Zane for saying that. I even hated Maizy for letting him do what he wanted with her, like she was trash. I wished I was home in my own bed, and not on this creepy bus. The minister was snoring with his Bible open on his lap, and I pretended I was asleep. I didn't want to talk to Zane any more that night.

CHAPTER 14

Fred

It was two o'clock when the buses from the United Church of God lumbered into the parking lot of the Lake Baraboo Lodge in the Wisconsin Dells.

"Praise God." The Reverend's voice boomed and the bus lights went on. "We've arrived. Everyone up!" Loud enough to wake the dead, Fred thought, but Zane and many of the passengers slept on. Fred shook Zane.

"Yeah? What?"

"We're here. The Dells," Fred said. He tried to be cool, not to sound excited. He leaned over Zane to look out the window. His first view of the Dells was the parking lot.

The Reverend was walking down the aisle, shaking shoulders to wake the sleepers.

The driver had opened the door, and Fred was first off the bus. He pulled the hood of his down jacket over his head. It was damn cold out. Patches of ice shimmered on the pavement under the light of a few dim lampposts. He looked up, hoping to see sandstone cliffs rising to the sky. No cliffs, but he'd never seen so many stars. The sharp lemon-wedge of a moon was bright as a hundred-watt bulb.

80

The cold air smelled clean and fresh after the sour breath stink on the bus, and he breathed big icy gulps. His stomach rumbled. He pulled half an Oh Henry bar from his pocket and bit off a chunk.

"Man, it's cold." Zane was at his side, and the passengers of the two buses stumbled out onto the parking lot. Kids whooped out of the second bus and raced around, as if it were the middle of the day. *So there are kids on this camping trip,* Fred thought.

A whistle shrilled and a voice, not the Reverend's, bellowed: "Quiet! Families get together."

Kids found their fathers. The gear from both buses was unloaded and piled onto the back of a truck. A guy wearing a long leather coat and an Indian headdress led them across the parking lot into the lodge, a huge room with log walls. Wheels of lights hung from the high ceiling. Two fireplaces blazed. Couches and chairs, cushioned in bright colors, looked so comfortable that Fred longed to drop onto one and sleep.

"Food!" Zane yelled. "I'm starved." A long wood-topped table in front of one of the fireplaces held pitchers of milk and juice, a big coffee maker, plates stacked with sandwiches. There were bowls for the steaming pots of cereal.

It was past three when Fred and Zane found the room matching their key number. It had log walls and two beds piled high with blankets. A door was open onto a connecting room.

"Shit," Zane said. "Dad's got the room next to us."

Through the open door, Fred saw the Reverend sitting at a table, taking sheaves of papers from his leather attaché case, stacking them in orderly piles. *Probably arranging his sermons,* Fred thought. *There's gonna be a lot of preaching going on.*

Reverend Caruthers came to the door. "Better get right to bed. Prayer call at six. Get on your knees and thank God for a safe arrival."

"Can we close the door, Dad?" Zane said.

"Don't lock it."

The announcement came over the loudspeaker: "Morning prayer will be offered in the chapel. Be ready to board buses at seven."

Fred opened his eyes. It wasn't even daylight yet. He wanted to bury himself under the blankets and go back to sleep. In the next bed, Zane's head was hidden under the covers. Fred was trying to get a look at his wristwatch when the connecting door opened and the Reverend came into the room, fully dressed in a black suit. Against the gray-black of the room, he looked like a spook, something left over from the night.

"Get up, boys. You have an hour to dress and eat breakfast before the bus leaves for the chapel."

"I'm not going," came Zane's muffled voice from under his blankets.

Fred was shrugging into his robe when the Reverend strode over to Zane's bed and yanked off the covers.

"I'm sick, Dad," he whined. "I don't feel good."

"Unacceptable. Ask God to help you overcome your weakness. Be on that bus." He returned to his room, closing the door behind him.

"Are you sick?" Fred pulled his robe tight around him. The room was freezing.

"Sick of him bossing me around, dammit. Sick of prayers and churches."

"What if we don't go?"

"He'll lock us in this room. We'll eat bread and water. And when we get home, he'll sell the car."

❖

The misty sun was a red blur on the horizon when, over an hour later, the buses chugged into the chapel parking lot and unloaded sleepy passengers. The square stone church, its frosty spire like a glistening pink finger pointing to heaven, seemed to stand in its own space in the world, a solitary building between river and forest. Its long narrow windows hadn't yet caught the dawn light, and they gleamed like strips of black mirror. Fred thought he had never seen anything so beautiful as the small church, the rushing, rose-tinted river splashing at the edge of its narrow lawn, and the black forest of tall evergreens behind it.

It was cold inside the church and stark, the walls between the windows plain gray stone. The pews were cushionless benches of polished yellow wood. The altar was made of the same stone as the walls, and held nothing but a wooden pulpit. A lamp hanging from the high ceiling threw a cone of light on the pulpit, making it shine like varnish in the semidarkness of the church. Below the altar stood a small organ.

The early-morning light from the narrow windows threw silver stripes across the church. Fred compared it to others he'd visited in Chicago, when he'd been curious about churches. This one offered little comfort.

There were no more than two dozen people in the pews. The Reverend evidently hadn't succeeded in getting most of his congregation out of their beds for morning prayers. Fred and Zane took seats at the rear, but a stern look from the pulpit, where the Reverend had taken his place, a severe black Ichabod Crane-like figure, summoned them forward.

"No chance of sneaking out," Zane whispered.

The sermon and prayers were followed by half-hearted hymns from the mouths of the sleepy congregation, unaccompanied by music. The organist hadn't appeared either.

When the worshippers left the church, the red-gold sun no longer rested on the horizon and the air seemed warmer. Fred took a window seat on the half-empty bus, and he marveled at the huge cliffs soaring to the sky. The sunlight coated their sides like a strawberry milkshake spilling over them.

"They're full of caves," Zane said from his own window seat. "Indians still live there."

Saturday afternoon, the kids piled into the Lake Delton Steamboat for a cruise down the Wisconsin River. An Indian guide lectured about the history of the Dells. Five hundred million years ago, it had been the sandy beach of an ancient sea. Waves and winds had formed the sand into hills, which piled on each other to make the huge cliffs. Iron and other metal deposits in the sand kept the cliffs from crumbling as the winds whipped them into their fantastic, ever changing shapes.

Tribes of Indians, the guide said, had made their homes in the caverns and caves, and they had left behind huge burial mounds. Pictographs on the walls of the mounds showed their life through the ages. Ho-Chunk Indians, descendants of the original tribe, still lived in small reservations along the Wisconsin River. There were tours of the caves for anyone interested in seeing them. Fred was interested. *Someday,* he thought, *I'm coming back.*

Zane dozed in his seat as Fred moved from one side of the boat to the other, awed by the weird, wind-sculpted shapes of the huge cliffs. One was a giant mushroom; others rose like twisted fairy-tale castles into the sky. The clear river reflected them, distorting their already bizarre shapes into shivery ghost-towers. He wished he'd brought his sketchpad. He hoped he could remember the colors, every shade of red, beige, white, and brown. And all along the shore, in front of the cliffs, were deep, mysterious-looking forests; the trees, dark green, gray, smoky blue rising skyward, were silhouetted against the cliffs.

Zane was right, Fred thought, *about the church kids being jerks.* They raced around the boat, tussling with each other, yelling at the top of their voices, paying no attention to the lecture or the scenery, until the guide finally blew a whistle and ordered them to sit down. A girl he'd seen at the lodge came to stand beside Fred.

"Is this your first time at the Dells?" she asked. "I know a lot of the church kids from school. I live near Zane. We go to his father's church. I'm here with my folks."

"I'm a friend of Zane," he said. "He invited me."

"The minister's son. He's a real creep. Nobody likes him."

"Why not?"

She shrugged her pointy shoulders. "I dunno. He's a smart-ass, I guess. Hangs around with losers. Everyone says so."

"Well, then I'm a loser. He's my friend."

"Oh. No offense." She raised her eyebrows, as if surprised that Zane actually had a friend, and to Fred's surprise, she even blushed.

She had long, flippy hair, a stringy body, wore glasses. Her name was Hannah, she said.

"What's yours?"

"Fred. Fred Fink."

"For real?"

"What d'you mean, for real?"

"Well, it's a—peculiar name, that's all. Like a Disney character. Mickey Mouse, or Donald Duck."

He said nothing, remembering the Rev's comments. Maybe someday he'd change his name.

"How about hanging out with me, Fred?" she said. "There's a party after supper. We can ditch it."

"I'm with Zane. Can you get a girl for him?"

"No way," Hannah said, "I told you no one likes him."

"But everyone likes his pa, don't they?"

She shrugged again. "Well, our parents do, I guess. The kids think he's weird. Keeps to himself a lot. Doesn't mingle. Preaches at everyone. My folks say he's a righteous person, very moral. Not like the one before him, who went for the ladies even though he had a wife."

What a loser his wife must've been, Fred thought.

"So, what about tonight? You gonna be my date?"

"Nope. I guess not. Like I said, I'm here with Zane."

"Well, you're missing something, Fred Fink." She puckered her lips and ran her hands down her skinny body, sticking out her chest.

"Not interested," Fred said. "Sorry."

"Suit yourself."

He was glad when she walked away. Glad Zane wasn't there. He'd have taken her up on her offer. Himself, he just wasn't interested in girls that way, except as friends, like with Maizy. Zane and all the guys he knew were always talking about getting into their pants, never seemed to think of girls as people, just as lays.

The guide was still talking, but Fred had lost the thread of his lecture. What was it about Zane that turned the church kids off? And he hated them, too, but why? They seemed okay to Fred. Just plain ordinary kids, after all, some of them jerks, but some looked friendly enough. Same as the kids on Kenmore, or at the hotel. Except maybe they had more money, better homes. All Fred could figure out was, maybe Zane was too fast for them, always talking about making it with girls. Or maybe it was just because he was the minister's son.

❖

"So what did she want?"

Zane must have seen the girl talking to him. "Nothing. Just talking. She belongs to your church."

"Well, stay clear of those girls. They're poison. You put a hand on them and they claim you screwed them."

"Ever happen to you?"

"No way," Zane said.

But Fred wasn't so sure.

CHAPTER 15

Fred

A large sign in the lobby of the lodge informed the young people returning from the steamship tour that the Ho-Chunk Indian tribe would hold a powwow in the evening. There'd be a barbecue at six, followed by ceremonial dances performed by members of the tribe. The announcement continued: *Enjoy storytelling around campfires on the lodge grounds after the ceremony. Fathers and sons wishing to sleep in Indian teepees, sign up at the registration desk. It will be necessary to provide your own sleeping bags.*

"It's supposed to be a big deal," Zane said. "My dad will reserve a teepee for himself and us."

"Great," Fred said, unsure how he felt about sleeping in a teepee with the Reverend. He'd pass on it, if he could. "But maybe it would be good if you and your pa were together, just the two of you. I can sleep in the room. I won't mind. Honest."

"No way are you getting out of this, Freddy. But don't worry. My dad sleeps like he's in his coffin. We're leaving the dumb teepee, soon as he falls asleep."

"Where are we going?"

"You'll see." Zane dug their thermoses out of their backpacks. "I'm going down to the commissary and fill these with hot coffee. Make sure our flashlights have good batteries, and put extra socks in the backpacks. I'll be right back."

That was it? Fred wondered what they were getting into. You never knew with Zane. Well, nothing he could do about it now. But he didn't have a lot of dough to spend on some kind of binge.

Tomorrow night they'd be home. One more night and one more day. He should call his ma. He'd told her he would sometime during the retreat. Their room had no phone, but he knew the Rev's did. He'd heard it ring a couple times. He knocked on the door. No answer. The Rev was probably busy with arrangements for the powwow.

The door was unlocked. The phone was on the desk. He was sure the Rev wouldn't mind if he used the phone to call his ma. He had to push aside some of the papers on the desk to get to it. The Rev's attaché case was open, spilling more papers and a big fat envelope.

While he was waiting for the front desk to get him an outside line, he flipped open the flap of the envelope. It was stuffed with photos. He pulled out a couple. Little girls. All naked. Had Zane had a little sister?

He slid some of the pictures out of the envelope, thinking he'd find some of Zane as a little kid. But no boys. Only naked little girls, maybe five to ten years old. Some just babies. Some blond, some dark. All flat chested. Too young to have boobs. But they were posing to show everything, back and front. Like a Miss America contest gone wrong, with little girls only.

Quickly, he pushed them back in the envelope. The pictures shocked him and he felt sick. His heart raced. Why would the Rev have dirty pictures of little girls? Only perverts had pictures like those.

There had to be a reason why the Rev had those pictures. Some damn good reason.

Fred felt like he was going to throw up.

"I can get you a line now," the operator said.

"Never mind. I'll call later." No way could he talk to his mother now. His voice would shake and she'd demand to know what was wrong.

He went back to his room, closing the connecting door. Should he ask Zane about the pictures? What if Zane didn't know? What if he did? He felt weird and shaky, like he had a fever.

Don't get your ass in a sling, he told himself. *It's probably okay.* There would be some really good explanation. He splashed water on his face and went to check the flashlights.

He'd wait for the right time to ask Zane about the pictures.

❖

Fred and Zane stashed their backpacks in teepee number six and dug in at the barbecue. Best thing about the Dells was the food. From the veranda outside the dining room came delicious smells of meat kebobs turning on the grill, hot dogs on a giant spit, and hamburgers sizzling. There was the mouth-watering smell of onions frying, spicy-sweet steam from a black iron pot of chili beans, corncobs revolving over an open fire and heaps of vinegary potato salad in pottery bowls. Some of the adults, including the Rev, stood at the long table helping to dish out the food.

"Come on," Zane said. "Let's dig in."

They filled their plates, went inside and found a table for two at the back of the dining room. Zane stuffed food into his mouth, washing it down with gulps of pink lemonade. Fred put relish and catsup on his hamburger, took one bite, and put it back on the plate. He wasn't hungry. His stomach felt queasy.

"Hey. You're not eating." Zane prepared a second hot dog. "This is really good grub. We never have anything like it at home."

"I ate a candy bar while you were filling the thermoses. Guess I killed my appetite."

"Well, you're missing some mighty good vittles."

❖

The tables were arranged in a circle, leaving space in the middle of the dining room. Four Indian braves in full dress danced into the circle, beating tom-toms. Others followed, men and women in beaded costumes and feathers, and the dancing began. The loudspeaker announced: "Rain dance." "Corn dance." "Harvest dance." "War dance." The drums beat and the Indians chanted as they danced.

"Phony stuff," Zane said. "I bet they never did those dances for real."

"I like it," Fred said. He'd forced himself to get into the mood for the ceremonial, putting the Rev's pictures out of his head.

When the dancing was over and the applause faded, the Rev called for their attention. The room fell silent.

"Let us thank the Lord," he said, his prayer voice filling the large room, "for bringing us to this place of beauty, for feeding us bountifully, and for allowing us to see some of the religious practices of this noble tribe. Let us always respect the beliefs of those who know other gods than ours."

"Amen," everyone shouted.

"The bus leaves for the chapel at seven tomorrow morning," he continued. "Fathers and sons are to go to your assigned teepees within the hour. Good night, and God go with you."

The grassy grounds of the lodge were covered with teepees. Small bonfires had been lit in the barbecue pits, and groups of kids and adults clustered around the fires, singing, telling stories, talking. Fred and Zane wandered among the fires, stopping for a moment to listen to a story or to grab a roasted marshmallow from the end of a stick. Fred thought he saw the girl from the boat sneak off into the darkness, hand in hand with a boy. *Could have been me,* he thought. *Glad it's not.*

The men and boys were entering the teepees.

"Father and son talks," Zane sneered. "Good you're here, or I'd be in for one of those."

"I shouldn't be in there with you and your pa," Fred said. He thought he might have liked being in a teepee with his own pa, talking about things. But he sure didn't want to be in there with the Rev.

"Don't take your clothes off," Zane said. "Zip your sleeping bag all the way up. When he comes in, we'll pretend we're asleep. He's not going to wake us up for some dopey talk."

Teepee six was one of the larger ones. The three sleeping bags on top of low cots took up nearly all the space in the teepee.

"We'll leave the middle one for my dad, nice and cozy. Soon as we hear him snoring, we sneak out. I'll go first. I'll cough. That'll be the signal."

"You'll probably fall asleep, Zane. And we'll end up here all night."

"No way. Get in quick, now. He'll be here soon. It's after ten, way past his bedtime."

Zane was right. The Rev came into the teepee soon after they got into their sleeping bags, flashed his light over them, doused it, sat on the edge of his cot, and sighed as he took off his shoes. Fred moved as far to the side of his sleeping bag, away from the Rev, as he could. The smell of his aftershave made him sick. Through slit eyes, he saw him take off his trousers and jacket and slide into the sleeping bag. He'd brought the attaché case with him and slid it under the cot. Fred wondered if the pictures were in the case. The Rev mumbled some words, probably praying, and in a few minutes started snoring. Fred tensed, waiting for

Zane to cough. If he'd fallen asleep, Fred would leave without him and go to their room to sleep. Damned if he was going to spend the night in a cot next to the Rev.

Then he heard the cough.

❖

"We're going to take a walk," Zane said. "When we come to the road, we'll use our flashlights."

"Where we going?"

"Town. It's less than a mile."

"What's there?"

"You'll see."

"Come on. Tell me."

"A strip joint, a couple arcades. At the truck stop at the edge of town." He pulled his thermos out of his backpack, unscrewed the top, poured a drink into the cup, and handed it to Fred. "Drink it. It'll warm you up."

"What is it?"

"Booze. Got it from the bar this afternoon. Bartender was busy helping set up the powwow. There's some in your thermos, too."

"You said you were filling them with coffee."

"No way."

It burned going down but after a few swallows, Fred felt his stomach settle. On the road, a few cars passed. Far in the distance, an arc of light glowed against the sky.

"That the town?" Fred asked.

"Yep. It's waiting for us."

They started to jog, their breath swirling around them

like halos of fog. From time to time, they sipped from their thermoses. When they arrived at the truck stop, Fred felt like he was flying. He wanted to shout, sing.

"Hey, I'm starved. Let's eat."

Zane laughed.

"You let all that good grub at the lodge go to waste."

They ordered double burgers, squinting their eyes against the glare of headlights. Fred wolfed his down. Ordered another. The waitress, a teenager with pimples, took their order for beer without blinking.

"Save your dough for the arcades," Zane said.

There were two of them: Flames of Hades and Balls of Fire. Both were packed. They waited in line to play the noisiest, flashiest games in the arcade.

"Where'd all these people come from?" Fred asked. "Little town like this."

"Saturday night. Whole town's out for fun. And tourists from the different lodges in the Dells come here. Not everyone's here on a stupid retreat."

Across the road from the arcade was a log building, its window outlined in purple neon. GIRLS GIRLS GIRLS read the twinkling sign.

"Should we try to get in?" Zane asked.

Fred's head was throbbing and his stomach felt sour. He kept belching the onions from the burgers. The blurry face of his watch showed one. He felt like he was skating on slippery ice and could fall down any second.

"We better get back," he said. "What if your pa wakes up and we're gone?"

"We'll say we had to take a pee."

Both roared with laughter.

"Know something," Zane said, "we're drunk."

"Tell me something I don't know. Your pa will smell it on us."

"We're not going back in the teepee. We'll say we got cold and went back to the room."

"Smart-aleck!"

They doubled over laughing. Fred hiccupped and tasted something bitter. He thought of the Rev's face when he woke up and found them gone. His lips would be squeezed and there'd be a mean scowl on his rat face. He couldn't remember why he hated the minister's guts so much. He was really a good old guy, letting him come along on this great trip. Fred loved the Dells.

CHAPTER 16

Fred

Somewhere on that dark cold road back to the lodge, I had to stop and barf. Thought my stomach would come up along with the booze and the food we'd eaten. Zane kept telling me to hurry it up, but every time I thought I was finished, more came up. When it was all over, I started shivering so hard I could hear my bones rattle.

"I gotta stay here," I said and dropped down on the shoulder of the road. My legs were weak as water. No way could I keep on walking back to the lodge. I just wanted to sleep right there, on the ground.

"No you don't," Zane said. "What if the sheriff comes by and sees us out here this time of night? He'll take us to the lockup. And they'll get my dad on us. He'll probably let us rot in jail."

Zane was right. I didn't want the Rev coming after us, or my ma finding out I'd messed up big-time. So I dragged myself up and, hanging onto Zane, finally got back to the lodge.

Back in our room, I dropped onto the bed without even taking off my shoes and fell into the king of all nightmares.

I was in a sea of worms, thick and gooey, trying to swim to the surface. The worms kept coming at me, in my nose, mouth, eyes, tangling in my hair. It was disgusting, sickening. They had faces of the Rev, Zane, my ma, even Maizy. I felt like I was suffocating in cold slime. The bang of a slammed door saved my life.

I woke up to see the Rev's stony face hanging above me.

"This will require an explanation," he said, his voice cold and sharp enough to draw blood.

I looked over at Zane, sound asleep. Was I getting blamed for whatever his pa knew about last night?

My head was spinning; my throat ached. My mouth was dry as sand.

"We came in because we were cold," I croaked.

"This room stinks of alcohol and vomit," he hissed. "It's six o'clock. Wake him up." He leaned over and gave Zane a punch in the back. But Zane didn't move. "Get yourselves into a hot shower and be on that bus for church at seven. You've got a lot of repenting to do. There'll be punishment to face later." He walked to the door connecting his room to ours. "Be on that bus. After church, we're heading home." He went into his room and closed the door with a bang.

Did he know what we did last night? Did he find out we went to town, or did he think we hung around here and got drunk?

No way was I going to miss that bus and get left behind. I'd had it with the Dells. I didn't want to be there a minute longer than I had to. I took deep breaths, squeezed my eyes shut, trying to stop the room from whirling, and pounded on Zane.

"Go to hell," he mumbled. I was glad to know he was alive.

"Get up or I'm dousing you with cold water." I kept up the pounding.

"Okay, okay, let up," he said. "Does my dad know we're here?"

"Oh, yeah. And we're in deep shit," I said. "We gotta be on that bus in an hour. It's heading for home after church. Now move your ass. We gotta shower and put on clean duds, and then figure out what to tell your pa."

Somehow we got cleaned up, packed our stuff, and got on the bus, just as the Rev was finishing praying at the passengers. Our front seats were taken so we sat in back. I was glad not to be under the Rev's eye. We didn't have time for breakfast, but just as well. My stomach was sour as a lemon.

At church, Zane dozed through the sermon. But I didn't dare close my eyes. The Rev was preaching to everyone but looking right at us—something about transgressions. I was too tired to follow what he was ranting about. I shivered in the cold church, and wondered how yesterday I could have thought it was beautiful.

At last, we were back on the bus. After stopping at the lodge to pick up the late sleepers who hadn't made it to church, we headed home. I noticed everyone had packages, probably box lunches. Zane and I had nothing. I had a few coins in my jeans pocket. I'd buy us some candy bars when we got to a rest stop. My stomach was beginning to rumble for food. Hot soup was what it wanted.

As soon as we got on the bus, Zane conked out. Somehow, I didn't feel sleepy. I went over last night in my mind. What had we really done that was so terrible? We'd known it was against the rules to leave the lodge, and getting drunk wasn't good, but was it a crime? *We should just confess,* I thought, *and take our punishment, whatever the Rev decides it should be.*

What could he do to me? Forbid Zane to see me? That wouldn't stop Zane.

He'd probably take the car away, and that would really be bad news. Zane loved that car. Yeah, he'd get the worst of it. But it was his idea.

I did go along with it, without objecting.

If I'd still had a pa, I'd just tell him what we did. He'd say it was dangerous, going to a strange town at night, and that getting drunk was stupid. You could get into all kinds of trouble. He'd say, "See you don't do it again." And that would be the end of it.

I didn't want my ma to know, though. Women are different about things like that. They don't understand boys so good. Ma would be real disappointed. She'd get depressed. Maybe start drinking again, like when we lived at the hotel, before she went to the counselor.

I looked at Zane. He was sleeping like he didn't have a care, and like he wasn't starving without breakfast. His light eyelashes lay on his pink cheeks like the soft bristles of one of my sable paintbrushes, and his heavy blond hair was scattered, with strands falling over his forehead. I thought he was beautiful. I wanted to push the hair back off his face, touch his cheek. His neck would be warm under the collar of his jacket. 'Course I didn't. But I wanted to.

His hands were clasped loose in his lap. I wished I were as handsome as Zane, with big shoulders and muscles in his arms and legs. *Wonder if he ever thinks about me like I think about him?*

I looked like my father. He was medium tall, thin, straight black hair, dark eyes squinting in the sun, and a nose too big for his face. In the pictures of him and Ma together, she looked happy, pretty. Now she was always on a diet, afraid she'd get fat like my grandmother.

I felt sorry Zane didn't have a ma. Maybe she'd stick up for him against the Rev. Having a pa that hates you is worse than having no pa at all.

Maybe the Rev didn't like boys much. Maybe he only liked little girls.

"Rest stop coming up," the bus driver bellowed. "Fifteen minutes."

I poked Zane.

"Let's get off," I said. "I gotta pee."

We lined up at the men's. Zane looked sleepy, didn't seem to feel like talking.

After we finished, I spent my last two quarters and got a couple of Hershey bars. We took long drinks at the fountain.

Back on the bus, people were opening box lunches. I smelled cheese, spicy pickles, coleslaw with mayonnaise, chicken soup. My mouth watered.

I handed one of the candy bars to Zane.

"No thanks," he said. He stared out the window. He seemed depressed.

"Are you worried about what your pa will do to you when you get home?"

"I guess."

"Why don't we just tell him the whole thing? It's not that bad. We didn't hurt anyone."

"You don't know my dad."

"Well, he *is* your pa, after all," I said. "He wants you to do good. We deserve to be punished."

"You'll get away with a lecture. You're not his kid. He can't do anything to you. Probably tell your mom you got soused. He hates me, and this will give him a reason to really let me have it."

"He doesn't hate you. He's your pa."

"Yeah, he does. Always has."

"Will he hit you?"

"Maybe. He'll for sure take away everything I got— radio, record player, the car for sure. Maybe even make me go to the parochial school."

"That seems pretty rough for what we did. What if I take part of the blame? I'll say it was my idea."

"Won't matter." Zane looked like he could cry, eyes red-rimmed. "Maybe I'll run away."

"My ma would probably take you in."

"No. He'd find me there."

"What if you had something on him he didn't want anyone to know?"

"Like what?"

Wait a minute, my inner voice warned. *Don't blab. Think about it first.*

"Like—I don't know, just saying, 'what if.' "

Zane turned toward the window and closed his eyes.

What about those dirty pictures the Rev had in his

case? I couldn't really remember that much about them; I didn't look that close, afraid he'd catch me. But they were naked little girls all right, back and front, everything showing. Little butts and all. Were they touching themselves? Each other? I couldn't remember. The high-and-mighty Rev really could be a pervert.

But did just having pictures in your briefcase make you a pervert? I didn't know. There could be a perfectly good reason he had them. Because he's Zane's father, I hoped there was.

Maybe Zane knows about the pictures and knows why his pa has them. Maybe he doesn't. Should I tell him? But that would put me in it, too. What if Ma ever found out?

I decided I wouldn't tell Zane about the pictures. I wouldn't tell anyone. Probably did wrong snooping at his private things. Invaded his privacy. Wished I could ask someone.

Zane was either asleep or just sitting there with his eyes closed. Let him sleep. I didn't want to talk anyhow. I looked at my watch. It was almost twelve. The bus had left the church in the Dells at nine, after the Rev had talked two hours at the chapel. It was a seven-hour trip back to Chicago. Meant we wouldn't be there until four o'clock— four more terrible hours. I wished I could go to sleep. Most of the passengers were sleeping, even the Rev, up front. He had his case on his lap, as if to be sure no one would get hold of it.

I buried my head inside my jacket and closed my eyes. But in my mind, I kept seeing pictures of those little girls.

Wished I knew what to do. Wished I'd never gone on this trip to hell.

CHAPTER 17

Maizy

Maizy was worried. Something had happened to Zane. Maybe he was sick. Maybe his father sent him away to Iowa, like he was always threatening. She'd waited every afternoon, hoping he'd come by after school. She knew he would if he could. She wanted to see him so bad, and she knew he wanted to see her. Last thing he'd said when she got out of his car after they'd done it was "see you."

She was *sure* he'd said that. Hadn't he? She hoped he'd meant it. He hadn't even been at the shack since then to see his buddies. She'd asked Marko and some of the others, but they hadn't seen him either.

Fred Fink passed her house on his bike several times on his way to the grocery or wherever, but he hadn't stopped to talk to her, not since that day at the hydrant, and that was over two months ago. He was mad at her—she knew it. It was because Joey told that Pa had hit her. Fred must've thought it was because she had been bad, and he didn't want anything to do with a bad girl. Or maybe Fred found out about her and Zane—Zane could've told him. She wanted to explain to Fred about her and Zane. She was his girl. Fred would understand that when you're in love, of course, you're gonna do it. But Fred kept avoiding her, so how could she tell him?

She was irritable with Joey, and bored being home by herself every day when Joey was at school. She was never very smart, but she sure missed school. It was lonesome at home all day, with no one to talk to. She had the feeling that if things didn't change soon, she'd just go crazy.

She'd baked cookies and brought a plateful to Z's one morning. Left it outside the door. She'd planned to go in and look for the bra, but the door was locked.

She never heard from anyone about the cookies.

I should take a walk, she thought. *I'm putting on weight, eating all day, cookies and candy.* Every night she made a big dinner for Joey and her pa, and she ate it with them. She was always hungry. Now she could hardly fit in her clothes, her stomach was getting so big.

It was eleven o'clock in the morning. Joey was at school, all the beds were made and the house dusted. Yesterday was washday, so she didn't have that to do. *I'll walk over to the park,* she decided. That guy she'd seen in the lav hadn't come around anymore. She'd stopped being afraid of him.

It was a beautiful day, Indian summer. Real warm with a little breeze that blew the remaining leaves off the trees. They lay on the park lawn like a carpet, red and gold, and crackly. Too bad they'd have to be raked up.

Some mothers were on the benches, some pushing babies in strollers, playing with little kids in the sandbox or on the swings.

On one of the green-painted park benches, Maizy saw Anna Carney, the murdered girl's ma, watching the children play. She looked just like a teenager—thin, in jeans and a yellow T-shirt. Her hair was straggly, as if she didn't bother to comb it when she got up in the morning. Her face was pale and tired.

"Hey!" Maizy sat on the bench beside her. "Remember me?"

"You got fat," Anna said.

"Yeah, and you got thin." She giggled at the joke she'd made. "Here, have an Oreo." She dug a package of cookies out of her big bag.

Anna took one, but she held it in her lap while Maizy split hers and licked the creamy filling.

"Do you come to the park a lot?" Maizy asked.

Anna shrugged. "Yes, I guess so. Nothing else to do when Josef works. Do you not go to school?"

Maizy felt her face go red. "I had to drop out. I take care of my little brother. He's at his school now. I have to pick him up later."

"But you could go to school—"

"I don't want to," Maizy answered quickly, not to give the ache in her heart time to get started. "Maybe next year I'll go back. My boyfriend will be in college then."

"You have a boyfriend?"

"Yes. We're in love. Someday we'll get married. How long have you been married?"

"Josef and me, we married just before Marta was born. Over five years. Marta was only five when . . ." Tears welled up in Anna's pale eyes. "Only three months ago, she played here in the park."

Maizy took a tissue out of her bag and handed it to Anna.

"You miss Marta a lot, don't you?"

"Of course. Josef, too. A child dies, it's the end of the world for the parents."

"Not if they have another," Maizy said.

"Josef and me, we—don't lie together anymore. He is so—I don't know how you say it. Uneasy, maybe. But more. The hand, Marta's hand is missing. He cannot go on with his life until the hand comes back."

Maizy remembered how the child had been found in the lake, the right hand missing. The police had looked and looked for the hand. It seemed like a long time ago, the beginning of summer.

"Well," Maizy said, "I'm going to have a lot of kids. Me and Zane. That's my boyfriend. I like kids."

"Your brother? He is disabled?" Anna asked.

Maizy laughed. "Not really disabled. He can do everything all kids do. Just he's a little slow. Sometimes he's a real handful. Hey, you didn't eat your cookie. You should eat more. You're awful thin."

"Will you mind if I say something?"

"Nope. Say anything."

"You should not eat cookies. It is not good to be too—"

"Yeah, I know what you mean. I'm going to the clinic and get some pills to make me thin. Mind if I say something to you, Anna? You won't get mad?"

"No. It's all right. Say."

"Well, I think you should get a job. It's depressing sitting in the park all day watching other people's kids. You could get a job at the grocery, meet some people that way. Or take care of some kid whose ma works. All kinda things."

"Josef will not allow me to work. He is too proud."

"Oh. Well, too bad. Anyway, I gotta go now. Time to start cooking and then pick up Joey. See ya soon, okay? We can be friends if you want to."

"I'd like that," Anna said.

❖

Next morning, after she'd brought Joey to school, Maizy sat at the kitchen table with a pencil and a page from Joey's scratch pad. She'd baked cookies the night before, when Joey was in bed, to take to the shack like she'd done before, but this time she would leave a note for Zane. She'd give him her telephone number—*I should've done that the last time, she thought.*

Dear Zane, she wrote. *I hope you are well. I am fine. I miss you. I think of you all the time. I hope you like the cookeys I made. You can share them with your friends. I know I shud not come here to your pryvat place, but I did not know any way to reech you. I will never come when enyone is there. If you find my bra, you cud keep it for when we see each other. I miss you, I love you. love, Maizy p.s. here is my fone #.* She wrote the number large at the bottom of the page.

On the sealed envelope she wrote: *Pryvat,* to *Zane.* She left the cookies and the note on the step.

❖

Then she walked to the clinic. It was squeezed in between the shoe store and the laundry. And usually there was a line waiting to get in, but not this morning. Inside, the seats were all taken. Maizy signed the waiting list. *I'll go home and make the beds,* she decided. *When I come back, it'll be my turn.* But on her way out, the nurse at the desk called her.

"Dr. Taylor can see you now," she said. Maizy knew who Dr. Taylor was. He took care of the girls at school who got in trouble. Maybe he was the one who gave out diet pills, too.

"I need some pills to lose weight," she told the nurse. "I'm always so hungry. Seems I never can get filled up."

She put on the short gown the nurse handed her. It barely tied around her waist.

"Why do I need to get undressed for diet pills?" she asked.

"The doctor won't prescribe anything without an examination."

The nurse took some blood and had her pee in a little paper cup.

❖

"When did you last have relations?" the doctor asked.

"Relations?"

"Sex." The doctor sighed. "Do you have a boyfriend?"

Maizy blushed. "I don't have sex," she said. "I have a boyfriend. We did it once. It was my first time."

"Well," the young doctor said, "you're pregnant, miss.

I'd say about three months. On your way out, get instructions from the receptionist. You should lose some weight. It'll be better for the baby. Eat fresh vegetables and fruit. Get some exercise. Drink lots of water. Make an appointment to see me in a month."

"You can get dressed now," the nurse said. "Hurry. There are patients waiting."

Maizy was stunned. She had a baby inside her, Zane's baby. A rush of love rolled over her like a warm ocean wave. She and Zane were going to have a baby. Their own baby to love forever. She dressed as if in a dream. Zane's baby was growing inside her.

By the time Maizy left the clinic, the euphoria she'd felt had turned into panic. How could she and Zane take care of a baby? Would Zane quit school and get a job? Or would he even want the baby? What would his pa say? What would her own pa say? He would throw her out for screwing around. *That's* what he'd say. Then who would take care of Joey? All the joy she'd felt in the doctor's office about carrying a beginning baby, Zane's and hers, melted into a pool of fear and doubt. She walked home. In her room, she pulled the shade against the daylight and lay on her bed. She cradled her abdomen with her hands. *My baby, my little baby,* she thought. She could see him. He had Zane's thick sandy hair, his sharp blue eyes. She loved him already.

But what if Zane didn't want their baby? How could she take care of it? She knew about abortions. Some of the girls at school had had accidents. Their boyfriends didn't want a baby, and neither did they. They'd taken care of it, and gone on with their lives. To Maizy it was like they'd killed the little baby. *I couldn't do that,* she thought. To her, the beginning life inside her already had a soul.

God, she prayed, *tell me what to do. Help me to do the best thing for my baby.* The little prayer made her feel much better. God would help her. When the right time came, she'd tell Zane about their baby. Maybe God would find a way for them to take care of him.

Feeling lighter in her heart, she fell asleep.

CHAPTER 18

Maizy

When Maizy woke from her nap, it was way past lunchtime. Her stomach felt hollow. She took the bowl of leftover macaroni from the fridge, poured a glass of milk, and ate the whole thing. It would have been enough for supper for all three of them, with a can of soup and a salad, but now it was gone, and she'd have to go to the store for something to cook. She'd better hurry—it was almost time to get Joey from school.

Maybe Zane came by while she was asleep. Well, he should've rung the bell. She patted her stomach. *Wait'll he hears what I got in here,* she thought. She hoped he'd be glad. Not like Agnes's boyfriend, who was so mad he beat her up when she told him they were going to have a baby. No, Zane wouldn't hit her. His pa was a minister and raised him good. He was finer than the other boys, even if he acted tough to be like them. She could see it in him, the kindness he tried to hide.

Would the minister be mad that Zane was already going to be a pa? Would he have to give up going to college? They'd be young parents, not even eighteen when their baby got born.

Maybe Zane wouldn't want the baby, tell her to get rid of it.

I won't do that, Maizy thought. *Never.* "Don't you worry," she said to the little life inside her. "Nothing's going to hurt you. God will figure things out. I'll pray every day."

She hurried to the store to buy lettuce and bread and some meat for hamburgers. Pa was good about giving her enough money for food. She bought very little for herself, She saved some every day and put it in the bank. Pa didn't know. It was her secret. Made her feel good to know that if Pa got laid off, or someone got real sick, she'd have some money put by.

"Don't save on food," he told her. "We need to eat good to stay well." She bought good food, but she bought it on sale whenever she could.

She went to get Joey, and when they got home, she put Oreos out for a snack. He took his cookies to sit in front of the radio. He loved the afternoon kid programs.

"You should play outside," she told him.

"My shows are on," he said. "I gotta listen."

Well, she said to herself, *let him listen. No one wants to play with him anyway.*

She sat on the step, watching the kids getting home from school. They were yelling to each other across the street, bouncing balls against the steps, coming out of their houses with sandwiches and paper cups of milk, a bat under their arm or a softball, on their way to call for a friend to go to the park. She felt bad for Joey. If they'd give him a chance, he could learn to bat a ball or even pitch. And he loved to play with other kids.

Was that Fred coming down the street on his bike? She wondered if he'd pass her by. She got up from the step.

"Fred," she called when he was a few houses away down the street. She waved both arms. Now he'd have to stop.

He pulled up in front of her house.

"Hi," she said.

He looked at her hard, straddling his bike. Put his hand in his jacket pocket and pulled something out—her bra.

"This yours?"

She felt her face grow hot. She reached for it.

"Where'd you get it?" she asked, but she knew. Zane must've given it to him. "Why're you carrying it around?" Had he shown it to his friends to make fun of her? She never thought Fred was that mean.

"What were you doing at the shack?"

"Zane took me," she said.

"Yeah? What'd you do there? Play strip poker?"

"We're in love, Fred."

"Yeah? Who says so? Not Zane."

"He wouldn't say. He's shy about it. We're lovers now."

"Doesn't sound shy to me. Anyone watching?"

" 'Course not."

"How'd you know no one would come in? Guys can walk in anytime."

"Well, no one did. Maybe Zane locked the door."

"It's not supposed to be a make-out place. No one brings girls there."

Why's he sound so angry? she wondered.

115

"He took me for a ride in his car, to show it off. We ended up there. We started to just make out, like we done before, and he lost control. He didn't know it was my first time."

"Oh, yeah? Why'n't you stop him?" He was standing with his legs on either side of his bike, one foot on a pedal, ready to take off. "Here. You're probably gonna need this someday." He threw the bra at her. It had been dangling from his hand. She picked it up from the step and put it behind her.

"I couldn't stop him, Fred. He was so excited. But it's okay, because we love each other."

"No, you don't. Least, he doesn't. Hasn't been around to see you, has he? Guy loves a girl, he comes to see her."

"Did he tell you we did it?"

"Sure. No big deal, he said. You think you're the first girl he's had?"

Maizy tried to keep her tears from falling. She wiped her face with the hem of her shirt. Her pa's old shirt. Hers wouldn't button over her stomach anymore, she was getting so big. Putting on more weight every day, it seemed.

"I love him, Fred. Always have, since we were little." She wiped her eyes again. The tears wouldn't stop. "It's different with us, Fred, Zane and me. Know why? I got his baby inside me. Our baby." She looked up at him. Her eyes kept tearing. She wiped her nose on her bare arm.

"The jerk didn't use a rubber?" Fred looked shocked. He let his bike fall to the sidewalk and sat down next to her on the step. He took out a mess of tissues from his pocket and handed them to Maizy.

"Here. They're clean, just wrinkled. Are you sure? About the baby, I mean." Now his voice sounded different, not so mad. More like he cared.

"I went to the clinic."

"Did you ask about getting rid of it?"

"I'm not gonna kill it. Zane wants this baby. We love each other. We'll get married."

"Maizy," Fred said, "you're a fool. Even if Zane loved you, he'll never tell his pa he got you in trouble. He'll never marry you."

CHAPTER 19

Fred

I moved over on the step, closer to Maizy, and put my hand on hers. It was balled into a fist over the tissues I'd given her to wipe her eyes. I suddenly felt so sorry for her. I know how it is, when everything is against you and there's no way out. I wanted to put my arms around her and tell her it would be all right, like my ma did when the hotel kids ganged up on me, called me a Jew fag. I'd been fighting them off ever since we came to the hotel, and I just couldn't stand it anymore. I'd lost it and run to our room, then started bawling like a little kid. Ma gave me a big hug.

"It'll be all right," she said, and even if I didn't know how it ever could be, it made me feel better.

Maizy didn't have a ma.

I was so mad at Zane, the rotten jerk, having his fun and not even thinking he could be wrecking someone's life.

"Oh jeez, Maizy," I said. "I'm sorry for you. You should think about getting rid of it. Girls at the hotel were always getting knocked up. Some younger'n you. We could tell my ma and she would know where to go."

Maizy pulled her hand away from mine. Her teary face got real red, and her eyes blazed like blue fires.

"I gotta go in now. It's late and Pa will be home soon. I don't need you feeling sorry for me, Fred Fink," she said. "Or telling me to kill my baby. Just tell Zane I need to see him, that's all I want from you." Then she slammed the door behind her.

She was mad at me, but she should be mad at Zane.

Lights were going on in the houses on Kenmore, and moms were calling their kids to come in for supper. I got up from the step, then pulled my bike out of the bushes where it fell when Maizy told me about the baby. I felt lonely and sad and angry, all of it mixed up in my mind. Should I tell Zane? Tell him Maizy needed to see him? That he'd knocked her up? I knew what he'd say—that it wasn't his, that it could be anyone's. That Maizy was a slut, and that he wanted nothing to do with her or her problems.

After the Dells, Zane's pa punished him by taking away the keys to the car, and warned him that he'd better watch it or he'd be sent to live in Iowa with his aunt Elaine and uncle Leroy.

"Would you hate that?" I asked him. He'd come to the table in the school lunchroom where I was eating alone, as usual.

"It would be hell," Zane said. "They live in this burg, Wicksbury, about five thousand people, surrounded by farms. My uncle's got a farm store, and all they do is work in that store and go to church. It's where my dad grew up."

So Zane's trying not to mess up, or so he said. He'd been real tight-assed, keeping to himself most of the time, so we didn't talk a lot.

That day he told me that his pa is sick.

"He could die," he said. "It's real bad. Happened all at once."

"What is it?" I asked, but he wouldn't say.

I knew Zane didn't like his pa that much. I was surprised how worried he seemed. It was just after Maizy told me about the baby, so I just couldn't bring myself to give him Maizy's message. It'd just be more bad news.

After that, I'd see him at the shack a lot of afternoons after school. We'd work on comic strips. He wanted to know how I got my ideas for *Fly Man* or *Ziplock*, two of the strips I do. Just think them up nights before I go to sleep, I told him. He's a pretty good artist himself. Does great caricatures. Sports figures like Ted Williams, and a great one of FDR smoking a cigar.

"Are you going to be an artist?" I asked him. "When you finish college?"

"I'm not going to college," he said.

I was flabbergasted. "If you didn't go to college, what would you do? Work as a bagger in the A & P market?" He didn't have any special skills like fixing cars or anything else. Except drawing.

"I want to go to the Art Institute instead of college. That's what I want to do," he said. "Anything wrong with that?"

"No. It's great," I said. "So do it."

"My dad won't pay for it. Says artists got bad morals."

"He wants you to be a minister, like him?" I asked. What I thought was, would a minister with good morals be carrying dirty pictures of little girls in his briefcase along with his sermons?

"Yeah, but he don't think I've got the brains for it. He's right. And I'd hate it. I got no call for preaching."

❖

One day, we happened to be at the shack by ourselves, Zane and me. It was Sunday, the day the other guys never showed up. He said the minister was in the hospital again for tests, so the coast was clear for him to go wherever he wanted. Usually on Sundays, he had to go to church and then hang around the house all day. I had had my sketchbook out and had been inking in a drawing when he came in.

"Wanna see something?" he asked. He plopped a thick brown envelope down on the table. I could've dropped dead. I knew that envelope. A few photos slid out of it.

"Take a look," he said.

I picked up a half dozen pictures. The same naked little girls in weird positions that I'd seen in the Rev's room at the Dells, showing all their parts. I tried not to let on how freaked out I was.

"Where'd you get these?" I asked.

"Found them in an empty locker at school. Just laying there."

I knew he was lying. Covering up because he'd never want anyone to know his pa had pictures like that.

"Why would someone want to look at these?" I asked.

"To jerk off to," he said. "Want to?" He didn't look like he really wanted to, more like wanting to see what I'd say.

"Zane, I gotta go. My ma wants me to do some stuff for her," I said. I didn't want to look at those pictures again. They disgusted me. Why would anyone want to look at little girls like that? Much less get sexed up by it? Why would the Rev? For the millionth time I wondered why he even had them. Maybe he took them away from some kid and put them in his case, meaning to get rid of them. That's what I wanted to believe, for Zane's sake.

Else, the Rev was a secret perv.

"Okay, go home to your ma," Zane said. "Pussy!"

I decided to ignore him calling me that. I gathered up my drawing stuff and left the shack.

"Close the door," Zane said.

CHAPTER 20

Maizy

"Damn you, Fred Fink." Maizy said it aloud as she peeled potatoes, tears and tap water flowing together into the sink.

Joey got to his feet. Dragging his unidentifiable stuffed animal and glancing over his shoulder at his comic books on the living room floor, he shuffled into the kitchen.

"What's a-matter, Maiz? You crying? What's a-matter? Huh?"

Maizy sniffed, wiped her nose on her sleeve.

"Nothing, Joey. It's okay. Go back to your books."

She bent to him, potato and peeler in her hands, and kissed his upturned face.

"You are such a sweet boy, Joey. I love you. Go look at your comics. Everything's okay."

But nothing was okay. Fred Fink said Zane didn't love her, but Fred was a liar. And a murderer, too, telling her to kill her baby. How had she ever thought Fred was her friend?

She had to get word to Zane. He would be so proud that he had made a baby. They'd name it after him: Zane

Junior. She'd write him a letter. Even if his father didn't let him come to Kenmore, Zane would find a way to see her.

I'll have to tell Pa soon, she thought. *Zane and I will tell him together. Pa won't hit me if Zane is there. And Pa can't throw me out because of Joey.*

But she knew Pa could hit her, even in front of Zane. And probably smack Zane, too, and then throw them both out. What would happen to Joey? Would Pa get someone to take care of him? Or put Joey in a "home"? When her ma died, Pa had said it was good she could take care of Joey, or he'd have had to put him in a home. A "home" was a place for children there was no one to take care of. It would be a sad place for a little boy like Joey, who didn't know how to play with other children and couldn't go to a regular school.

And when the baby came? How could she and Zane take care of a baby? It was on her mind all the time. Maizy's head ached. She put the potatoes into water with vegetables and stew meat and set the pot on the stove. Pa liked stew, and she had made cupcakes for dessert. A good dinner. She'd helped Joey with his bath, and he was in clean pajamas. She knew how to take care of a home and a little boy. She could take care of a baby, too, even if Zane wouldn't help her.

It will be all right, she told herself, and she went to play with Joey. The cooking stew smelled good, the house was clean, the table set. She began to feel better.

Soon she would be in Zane's arms again. A feeling of need, hot and wet, poured through her. Her panties were damp and her abdomen ached where the baby was.

She wanted Zane inside her again. It wouldn't hurt this time, and they would give each other pleasure. She squeezed her legs together and a wonderful throbbing shook her and left her feeling limp with relief. Had she groaned out loud? She looked at Joey to see if he'd noticed anything, but his eyes were on his book, his thumb in his mouth.

❖

After supper, Maizy put Joey to bed and read him a story from *Uncle Wiggily,* his favorite book.

"I'm tired, Pa," she said. "I'm going to bed now."

"So early?" Pa looked up from his newspaper. His glasses had slipped down his nose. He'd taken off his work shirt and his shoes, and she noticed with satisfaction how clean his white undershirt and socks were. She saw to it that he and Joey always had clean clothes to wear. He looked tired, but his serious thin face was quiet and peaceful. He had good hair, her pa, the color of rust, thick and wiry like hers. *I look like my pa,* she thought, *only I'm fat and he's thin.* He was a good pa, working hard to take care of them and not having much for himself. She was afraid of his anger, but she knew it was because he wanted her to be a good girl.

"I might go out for a while," he said. "Leave your bedroom door open in case Joey wakes up."

She'd been in bed a few minutes when she heard the front door close. Pa had gone out to be with his friends. The dark house was full of familiar creaks, and the October wind rattled the windows. Leaves rustled in the gutters just outside her room. Pa would be on a ladder Sunday, cleaning them out. She felt safe and optimistic. Nothing bad was going to happen. Her hands were between her legs and she held off touching herself, enjoying the anticipation of the pleasure she was about to feel.

❖

It had rained in the night. Indian summer was over. The morning air was cold and damp and smelled of the lake. Maizy put a sweater on Joey under his jacket. She walked him to his school, and on the way home, she cut through the park. It was empty of mothers and baby buggies, the benches slick with last night's rain.

She passed the men's lav and glanced in the open door, remembering the day she'd seen the man in there with the little girl. He was the same man she'd seen one day, walking on Kenmore, wearing a business suit. She'd never told anyone. He never came back. She'd almost forgotten the whole thing.

"Maizy?"

It was Anna. She'd come up behind her. She wore soiled jeans and a dark green sweater, and she looked cold and tired.

"I was going to the grocery store for coffee. What're you doing?"

"Nothing. I'll go with you."

On the way, Maizy told Anna about the man and the little girl in the lav.

"When?" Anna asked.

"Can't remember the date. It was sometime early last summer."

"My God!" Anna stopped walking, put her hand on Maizy's arm. "Did you tell the police?"

"No. He wasn't doing nothing, just standing there."

"Did you see the little girl?"

"Not really. Just the back of her. Why?" Maizy asked. "Probably a kid from around here. Maybe his own kid."

Anna put her hand over her mouth. She glared at Maizy. Her eyes burned like lumps of coal in a lit barbecue pit. Her face was tight and pale.

"What?"

"Marta."

Maizy's heart clenched.

"You mean—no, it wasn't Marta. It wasn't. It couldn't've been."

"You should've told the police." Anna didn't sound mad now, just very, very sad. "Maybe if it was Marta, they could've saved her."

"Oh, Anna . . ."

"Well, it happened. The police still look for who killed Marta. I go many times to the station and they say still they look. Nothing else we can do. Nothing brings Marta back."

Anna sounded so hopeless. Not angry with Maizy for not telling the cops, just very sad. *She's been over it in her mind,* Maizy thought. *She knows Marta's gone forever.* Poor, poor Anna. She wanted to take her in her arms and they would cry together. But Anna walked on, stiff and cold, like she didn't want to be touched.

At the grocery store, they carried steaming cartons of coffee to the back of the store where there was a counter and a few stools.

"Anna," Maizy said, "you should have another baby."

"You're a foolish girl, Maizy," Anna said. "People don't have another baby to take the place of one they lost."

They sipped their coffee in silence for a few moments.

"Josef—he looks for Marta's hand all this time," Anna said. "After months, he still looks. He walks near the lake where Marta was found, and looks and looks, under the rocks, in the sand. He says the lake will give back the hand."

"Anna . . ." Maizy didn't know what to say. She put her arm around Anna, but Anna shrugged it off, as if she didn't want Maizy's comfort or pity.

"Me and Josef," Anna went on, "we don't, like you say, screw anymore. Josef has only one thought, to find Marta's hand. The clinic worker says he's obsessed. Josef says if we stayed in Kentucky, we would still have Marta. It's no good here in Chicago."

"Why did you come?"

"So Josef could get work, and so we could send Marta to a good school. She was only five, but smart. We could see that."

"I'm so sorry for you, Anna. I wish I could help you."

Anna put her empty carton in the trash basket.

"There is no help for us," she said. "We just wait for the next day and the next. That's all."

Maizy followed her outside.

"Josef doesn't work today. He walks by the lake."

❖

Back home, the breakfast dishes were still in the sink, the beds unmade, but Maizy tore a page of notepaper out of one of Joey's copybooks and sat at the kitchen table. She'd write a letter to Zane. She'd have to ask Fred to give it to him. She'd never meant to talk to Fred again, but there was no other way. Leaving it at the shack was no good if he didn't go there anymore, and if she mailed it to his house, the minister might see it and tear it up.

Dear Zane, she wrote. *I hope you are well. I am well and happy. If you call me up or come to my house, I will tell you some good news. It is very important for me to see you. Please answer this letter. Your lover, Maizy*

After she'd folded the letter, she opened it again and added her phone number.

She put the letter in one of Pa's envelopes and sealed it.

She knew how to find Fred. He had a job after school now. He worked at the grocery market. She'd seen him there when she shopped.

CHAPTER 21

Maizy

Maizy, holding Joey's hand, entered Jewel's, the market where Fred Fink worked after school. She took a cart, and with Joey hanging on because he was eight and too big to sit in the child seat, she went up and down the aisles, selecting things she needed to make supper. There were a lot of people waiting to pay. She found the counter where Fred was bagging, and she took her place behind a mom with a baby who was buying a lot of groceries.

"Joey," she said, "stand behind me." She gave him a donut from the box she was buying. He was such a good boy. He'd stand and wait patiently while everyone ahead of them paid. Other children ran around the store, took candy off shelves and made nuisances of themselves, but not Joey. She sighed. He was so good, but sometimes she wished he were like other little boys. Then he'd grow up, be able to get a job, find a girl to marry, and she wouldn't have to take care of him all his life. Pa expected that of her, and she knew that, no matter what, she'd do it. She loved him so much. She turned and hugged him to her. She would soon have two babies to care for.

The line was slow because some people had food stamps and it took a lot of time to figure them out. *We're lucky,* she thought. *Pa has a job and we have plenty of money for food.*

What would Pa say about the baby? She thought about it all the time. He'd be mad, she knew that, but he wouldn't put her out, because of Joey. If Zane wanted to get married, maybe Pa would let him live with them. Zane could get a job and help with the money. But if Zane wanted to go away to college, she'd take care of their baby until he was finished. *All kinds of things can happen, so why worry?* Maizy told herself.

The woman ahead of her finally got her food stamps sorted out and it was Maizy's turn. Fred looked at her like a stranger, and didn't return her smile.

"Hello, Fred," she said.

" 'Hello, Fred,' " Joey echoed, peeking from behind her.

"Hi, Joey." Fred smiled at him.

The clerk started ringing up Maizy's purchases.

"Fred, I need to talk to you," Maizy said.

"I'm working now." He began bagging her groceries.

"Please, Fred. I need your help."

Joey tugged at her sleeve. "I gotta pee, Maiz," he said.

"Joey, wait a minute. Fred?"

"Take five," the sales clerk said to Fred, looking from him to Maizy as he finished totaling the bill.

"I'll take you to the bathroom, Joey." Fred took Joey's hand.

"I'll wait by the fruit," Maizy said.

131

A few minutes later, they were back.

"Fred, please don't be mad at me," Maizy said. She tried not to sound begging. She took Joey's hand, hugging the bag of groceries to her chest.

"I'm working here, Maizy. Don't come around when I'm on my job. I'll get fired. We're not supposed to have visitors."

"The guy said take five minutes." Maizy put the bag on the floor at her feet, pulled an envelope out of her purse.

"Please, will you give this to Zane? Please?"

"I don't see Zane a lot anymore."

"But he's at school, isn't he?"

"Yeah, sometimes. His pa's sick. He misses a lot of school."

"Just give him this when you see him. Tell him it's very important." She thrust the envelope at him. She tried to hold back tears.

Fred folded the envelope, and put it into his back pocket. "I don't know when I'll see Zane."

"When you give it to him, tell him it's from me. It's very important. Please help me, Fred."

He looked around to see if anyone was watching them. "Don't cry now. I work here, you know. I have to get back. I said I'll give it to him."

Maizy wiped her eyes on her sleeve. Dammit, she never used to cry so easy. Joey was looking at her, worried.

"Thank you, Fred. Sorry to bother you. Come on, Joey. We gotta get home." She tied his hood under his chin and picked up her bag of groceries.

It was drizzling and already dark. Streetlights shone

on the wet pavement, and cars whizzed by, taking people home for supper. She tried to feel good that Fred took her letter. He would give it to Zane. He said he would.

It's the rain, she thought. *It makes me sad.*

Two girls came out of Walgreen's. She recognized them from school. One took a lipstick out of a paper bag, opened the cover, and, pushing back her jacket sleeve, stroked some on her wrist. Maizy watched the girls study the slash of lipstick as they walked in the rain, laughing, not caring if they got wet. Maizy felt a hundred years older than those girls, fat and frowsy, her hair kinking up in the rain. If they looked at her, they'd see a sad, fat woman carrying a grocery bag in one arm, and holding a little boy's hand. Not a young girl their age, with nothing to worry about but the color of a new lipstick. She had a baby inside her and a little boy to care for, supper to make, and the house to clean before her pa came home. Her face was wet with tears, but thank goodness Joey would think it was rain and not ask any questions.

She wanted to throw the damp bag of groceries in the street, drop Joey's hot, chubby hand, and run home. Take off her wet clothes and get into bed with the door closed, so she could cry and cry.

CHAPTER 22

Fred

When I finished bagging and signed out, it was after nine. It was raining, and I was beat, but I'd be home in five minutes and Ma would have supper ready. Then it was homework and bed. School, work, homework, bed—not a fun day, but after another year I'll be in college. Ma and I, we'll have enough saved up so I won't have to work the first year. She's great and I'm lucky to have her. Be nice if I had a pa, too, but if you can't have both, it's better to have a ma. If Maizy and Zane had mothers, they'd be happier kids.

When Maizy came to Jewel's with Joey, I was really pissed off. I had a right to be, too. Sure, I feel real sorry for her trouble, but when I tried to help her, she got mad and slammed the door in my face. What's so wrong with getting rid of a seed before it even gets to be a baby, if you're a kid yourself and can't take care of it? Maizy'd try real hard, but there'd be no way. Her pa wouldn't put up with a bastard baby. And Zane, if it's his, which she says it is and I believe her, would never admit it. He'd never marry a girl like Maizy, even if he actually loved her.

Now I got this letter to give him.

She's crazy if she thinks he'll go see her.

Zane's in deep shit himself, ever since the Dells. Plus, his pa has some mysterious sickness and it's scaring him. He looks real down all the time.

Since the day at the shack, when he showed me those disgusting pictures and lied about where he got them, I've stayed clear of him. Those were his pa's pictures all right. I remember the brown envelope, and I even recognized some from when we were at the Dells. Who'd put pictures like that in an empty locker, like Zane said? He lied. But why'd he want to show them to me anyway?

Zane's pretty messed up these days.

❖

Two days after Maizy came to Jewel's, I gave Zane her letter at school. He was at his locker when I got to mine.

"Zane," I said, "I got something for you," and I pulled the envelope outta my pocket. It was wrinkled and smeared from being carried around, but it was still sealed.

"What is it?" he said, not reaching for it.

"It's a letter." Couldn't he see that?

"Who from?"

"Maizy asked me to give it to you." I held it out to him.

"Don't want it. Don't want nothing from her." He pretended he was having trouble closing his lock.

"You should take it. Read it. She said it's real important."

He took the envelope, tore it in half, and then tore the two halves in half, and dropped it in the garbage can.

"What did you do that for?" I asked.

It hurt me to see it. She took the trouble to write the letter and bring it to me to deliver. It couldn't've been easy for her to ask me. It had to be about the baby, but he didn't know that. He went to his class without another word about it.

I went to the trash, picked up the pieces of the unopened envelope, and put them back in my pocket. It was none of my business, but I wanted to see what was in the letter.

I put it together that night after work. Turned out it didn't mention the baby, just asked him to come and see her, that she had something to tell him.

What was I gonna say to her? That Zane tore up her letter without even opening the envelope? I couldn't do that to her. She was crying in the store, looked real down. She must've known Zane wouldn't come through, but she hoped. I felt real sorry for her. She'll believe in Zane, no matter what. Maybe that's what real love is—believing in someone forever, even if the other person doesn't care.

After school the next day, I got on my bike and rode to the lake. I had to think about how I was gonna tell Maizy Zane didn't read her letter. I crossed Sheridan Road and went past Zane's house next to the church, the kind of gray stone house you'd expect a minister to live in. Even though it was still light out, the house looked dark and cold. Zane's car was in the driveway. Must piss him off, seeing it there every day and not being allowed to drive it.

He's grounded until forever, so he must have been home. I half thought to ring the doorbell and see if he wanted to be friends again. I have no other friends. The guys at school don't like me and I keep outta their way. I got the feeling that if I try to mix with them, I'd be in trouble.

Maybe Zane would be glad of company. It had to be pretty dreary in that house, with no radio and only Miss Verner, who he never talks to anyway. I really had nothing much against him. All he'd done was show me dirty pictures that made me want to vomit. That and the way he tore up Maizy's letter, after I delivered it to him, which was none of my business. They weren't good enough reasons to dump him when he was in trouble. Actually, whatever he's done, I really love Zane.

But I didn't ring the bell. I went on to the lake. I connect to it. It seems big as an ocean, and it's a lot like a person. It can be mad as hell, dark and wild, have a tantrum, beating against the rocks like it wants to smash them to gravel. Or quiet and shining like a smile. Someday I want to have a house right near a lake like this one, where there's no other houses and no cars going by, gas fumes dirtying the air. I'd bring my ma there, and Maizy and her baby, and Joey.

I parked my bike and went to sit on the rocks. The lake was in one of its in-between moods. It was getting dark out, and a little windy. Not enough to make surf, just small, quiet waves bumping against the rocks. The water was the color of a silver dollar.

I started to think about Maizy. She's a good person, kind and loyal. I love her, but not the same way I love Zane.

I know I'll never love a girl that way, but still I want to take care of her. When I'm a famous cartoonist and have plenty of money, I'll find her. And if she needs me, I'll be there for her.

I thought of the time last summer when I first met her and we went inside her place to make out so I could impress Zane and his pals. How stupid that was. What is Z's, anyway, but an old shack with a smelly couch in it and a dead kid's hand buried under a floorboard? Hardly anyone came there except Zane and me.

I remembered Maizy's soft, sweet body, and how she made me feel okay about shooting off all over her. Even though I got lit up, it wasn't about sex that day. Just about doing what Zane and the guys expected of me.

To Maizy, Z's is special because of Zane. I'd've thought she'd hate it after what happened there and the trouble she's in because of going there, but she still thinks of it as Zane's club, a private place he took her to because he loves her.

It was nearly dark. I went to get my bike and head for home when I saw this guy walking on the rocks, real close to the water. He had a flashlight and was looking for something down there, where the waves hit the rocks.

CHAPTER 23

Zane

Zane brought a chair and his sketchpad onto the balcony outside his room. Sailboats way out on the lake looked like the pictures he used to draw when he was a little kid, white boats on a blue-crayoned lake.

The sun was ready to set and the balcony was in shadow. The air coming off the lake was cold, almost too cold to be out on the balcony. It was only November, but you could feel winter coming.

He examined the cartoon strip he'd been working on. *Pretty good,* he thought. Not as good as Fred's, but he was learning from Fred. At least he had been, before he was grounded for messing up at the Dells. Now he didn't get to see any of the guys. He had to come home right after school. He'd gone to the shack after school once or twice, walked all the way there and then home, but it was taking a chance his dad would find out. Miss Verner reported the exact time of his arrival home. No radio, no records. "Spend your time doing homework," his dad said, "improve your grades."

Zane'd have gone bananas if it wasn't for working on

the cartoons every day, trying to improve his technique according to what Fred had taught him. He called the latest one Super Sniper Sam. Sniper Sam, face of a fox, body of Mr. America, aimed at his bad-guy victims from towers, tops of trees, mountain peaks, blasting them with a special rifle. It had a long, slim shaft, and it shot marble-sized flaming-glass bullets that exploded on impact. In that day's strip, Sam was on top of the Eiffel Tower. Zane could see he needed Fred's help drawing the tower. It just didn't look right.

He'd made Fred mad when he tore up the letter from Maizy. He was sure he knew what the letter said. That she loved him and all that junk. Wanted to see him again. She thought she owned him now, because she'd let him fuck her. She'd probably try to get him to marry her, might even threaten to tell his father he'd raped her. Who'd believe her, a slut with a hillbilly father and a retarded brother?

But he was surprised by the feeling of comfort the thought of Maizy's love gave him. Funny, the only person who really loved him was someone whose love he didn't want.

Zane sighed. He erased the gun in Sniper's hand. It had to be longer, look wicked. Yeah, his dad would believe her if she told. He'd believe anything bad about him. He was against Zane because he wasn't the kind of son he wanted. He didn't get along with the church kids or get top grades, and he wouldn't apply to theological school to be a minister. The only thing he wanted to do after he graduated was go to art school, but his dad wouldn't spring for it.

What his dad didn't understand was that he didn't do

good in school because he couldn't. He couldn't keep his mind on school shit. The kids from church who went to the parochial school hated him, always had, maybe because the minister was his father, maybe other reasons. The snooty girls didn't go for him, not that he cared. He just didn't fit in with church people.

He was glad his dad was too tight to send him to the parochial school. His dad'd gone to public school, and he said it was plenty good enough for his son, too.

Zane wet the stick of charcoal on his tongue, a trick Fred taught him to make a line softer, and sketched in Sam Sniper's girlfriend, Roxie.

At high school he'd made some friends, all kids living on Kenmore, not rich kids like on Sheridan Road. The public school kids were his type. Trash, his dad called his new friends. Losers. Forbade him to associate with them. Didn't stop him, though. He was happy for the first time. The guys liked him, wanted to be his friends, even looked up to him. To them, he was a regular guy with a hangout of his own, a car, and a girl crazy about him.

As for being a minister, it was something he just could never do. He believed in God somehow, but not his dad's God. He'd make a terrible minister.

I always disappoint him, Zane thought, shifting his chair to the part of the balcony still in daylight. *Maybe if he loved me some, I could be better.* It's dumb to do stuff you don't want to for someone who don't even love you.

For the fourth time, he erased the top section of the Eiffel Tower. Just couldn't get it to look right.

Only person ever loved him was Maizy, a slut. He

didn't want her love, and wished he'd never done it with her. Made her think she had a right to bring cookies to the shack, write him letters, that kinda shit. If his dad found out he'd had sex, 'specially with a tramp, it'd be the end. For sure, he'd be shipped off to live with Aunt Elaine, be stuck forever in that lousy town, and spend the rest of his life working in their dismal store.

He was worried about his dad's sickness, too. He never said if it was really bad, but Zane knew he'd been taking lots of medicines and going for treatments for a long time.

"What's wrong with you, Dad?" he'd asked him. "Are you getting any better?"

"When the right time comes, I'll tell you about it," his father said. That made Zane worry all the more. If his father died, then what would happen to him?

The sailboats were coming in. A wind must've come up on the lake. The boats were listing shoreward, still a long way out. He hoped they'd make it before night. Sometimes Coast Guard sirens out on the lake woke him up, when some boat was in trouble in the dark.

He'd been dreaming funny stuff lately, ever since he found the pictures in his dad's underwear drawer, where he'd gone to look for the car keys. He'd been feeling real low, thought of stealing the keys, getting in the car, and running it into the lake at Edgewater Beach. Or drive to Milwaukee and get a job as a dishwasher, and just disappear from the hassle of his life.

What were the pictures all about, he wondered? Why would his dad have dirty pictures, the kind some of the street kids used to trade for dope? Probably found them on some kid and confiscated them. He pitied that kid. His dad would punish the hell out of him. He put them back where he'd found them. Someday, when he was sure he wouldn't get caught, he'd borrow that pack of pictures and have a good look. He hoped his dad would hold on to them long enough for him to get his look.

It was getting colder out on the balcony. He closed his sketchpad, dragged the chair back into the room. Soon his dad would be home for dinner, so he'd better put the pad away. The last thing he needed was for him to see the cartoons.

He stretched out on his bed and closed his eyes.

The dreams he had were of naked women flowing through the air like floating dolls. He'd reach out to catch one, but she always got away from him. There was one even looked like Maizy, frizzy blond hair and blue eyes, and a big soft face. He woke up from those dreams jerking off. He dried the wet on his sheet with the old hair dryer he found in the junk closet. Took a lot of time and left a stain. If the maid noticed it, she never said.

It would be easy to let himself fall for a girl like Maizy. Men did that—fell in love with tramps. Toulouse-Lautrec went for prostitutes; cops went for hookers, too, sometimes. He thought of Maizy's body, smelling like Ivory soap, soft as a cloud, her warm, sexy lips. No matter what he said or what he did, she'd love him. A girl like that don't expect nothing from you, just loved you, regardless. Well, no way was she for him. His dad would throw him out.

Crazy thinking, he told himself, getting off the bed.

Trash. Slut. Dumb hillbilly. He took his history book out of his backpack so his dad would see him reading school stuff.

He missed seeing Fred at the shack. Why was he always doing something to piss him off, like tearing up Maizy's letter? Fred was the only guy at school he really liked. Marko called him a fag, but that was Marko, crapping on everyone. Fred was an okay guy, and a real friend.

"Zane." His dad was standing at his door, opened it without knocking. Just like he always did.

"Yeah, Dad. I'm going over my history. Test tomorrow."

"Good." His father came into the room, sat on the edge of the bed.

"What do you say I give you back the keys to the car?"

"You mean—really?"

"Yes. You've been punished by me. Now you'll have to make your own peace with God."

His dad looked funny. Real pale, looking like he had a bad headache, eyes red around the rims.

"Thanks, Dad." He was a good old guy after all. "When can I get the keys?"

"We'll see."

He knew his dad had something more to say. He was sitting on the bed, looking at the floor. He cleared his throat. Zane closed his book, waiting for whatever it was.

"Son, I'm going in the hospital for surgery tomorrow. It doesn't look good. Will you pray for me?"

CHAPTER 24

Maizy

"You're a strong, healthy girl, Maizy," the doctor at the clinic said. "You'll have a fine baby. Be sure to take your vitamins and exercise. You can get dressed now, but before you leave, please see Miss Adams, room 333. She's waiting for you."

"Miss Adams?"

"The social worker."

"But why? She's not gonna talk me out of having my baby. I already decided."

"It's the policy of the clinic to send unmarried pregnant teenagers for a conference with Miss Adams. She'll ask you some questions."

Miss Adams was talking on the phone when Maizy walked into the open door of her office.

"Please have a seat," she said, hanging up the phone. She opened a folder that lay on the desk in front of her.

"Hello, Maizy." She was a large woman wearing a white smock over a dark dress, not much makeup. Her dark-rimmed glasses were smeary. Her face was plain and serious; you couldn't tell if she liked you or not.

"Let's see, you've missed four periods. How do you feel?"

"Good, thanks."

"I'm glad you're keeping your appointments with the doctor. It's important for you and for the baby. You're not married?"

"No, ma'am. Not yet." Maizy tried to meet Miss Adams's eyes. She felt like this was some kind of a test. The questions made her nervous.

"Do you know who the father is?"

Maizy was shocked. How could she *not* know who the father was? You *had* to know who your baby's father was.

"Sure I do."

"Good. Some girls go with several boys. They aren't always sure."

"Well, I am. I only ever had one boy, and it was my first time."

"Is the father employed?"

"He goes to school. He'll graduate this year."

"How old is he?"

"Seventeen."

"Are you living with your parents?"

"My pa. Ma's dead."

"How does your father feel about your pregnancy?"

"He don't know yet." Maizy's heart jumped with fear. What would Pa say?

"I suggest you tell him as soon as possible. He'll have to come with you to your next appointment."

"He works, Miss." She couldn't imagine asking Pa to come here with her.

"We're open until nine."

"He works at night, too." Her hands were wet and she could feel sweat rolling down her armpits. If Pa had to get in on this, he'd never let her have the baby.

"Maizy, your father will need to come with you at your next appointment. We need to make sure the baby will have a place to live and will have good care. If he doesn't come, we must notify Child Welfare. They will see that you have a place to go until the baby is born, and will help you to place it."

"I'm not going to place my baby, Miss. Zane and I will get married when we can. My Pa will let me stay home till then."

"Wonderful. But we have to hear that from your father. Please stop at the desk to make your appointment. I'll see you in a month."

Maizy left the clinic without stopping at the appointment desk.

❖

She took the long way home through the park, hoping Anna would be there. They could go to the store and get coffee and talk. It would make her feel better to talk to another girl. But Anna wasn't in the park.

She'd have to tell Pa about the baby soon, and she didn't know how to do it. She'd wanted to tell Zane first, and they could face Pa together.

Maizy wondered if Fred gave Zane her letter. It was three days now, and she hadn't heard from either one. She'd hoped Zane would have come by now. But maybe he didn't get her letter yet. Or he could be sick and stayed home from school. Fred said his father was sick, so maybe he hadn't had time. Or Fred hadn't given the letter to him, though he'd promised, and she thought Fred was the type to keep a promise.

She had to find out. Only one way: go again to the store where Fred worked and ask him. He'd get mad. He'd said he didn't want her to bother him at work, but there was nothing else to do, no other way to see him. She'd go there before she picked Joey up and just stay a minute, just to ask him. He wouldn't even have to take a break.

At home, she finished making the beds and dusting. She had the broom out on the porch, sweeping up the leaves the wind blew over, when she saw Fred on his bike.

He pulled up to her house and leaned his bike against the porch.

"What are you doing here?" she asked. "Isn't there school?"

"It's my lunch hour," he said. "I came here to see you."

"Well, come in, I'll make peanut butter sandwiches."

"No, thanks, I brought my lunch from home."

He followed her into the kitchen, sat at the table, and unpacked his lunch bag. Maizy poured him a glass of milk and herself a cup of coffee from the pot on the stove.

"Fred, did you give Zane the letter?"

"Yeah."

"What'd he say?"

"Nothing."

"Well, did he read it or put it in his pocket to read later?"

Fred shrugged, took a bite of his egg sandwich, and washed it down with milk.

"He went on to his class," Fred said.

Maizy offered Fred an Oreo from the package she'd brought from the cupboard. He shook his head.

"Well, did he read it or what?" Her voice got impatient. She was beginning to think Fred was holding something back.

"Maizy, Zane's got a lot of trouble now. His father's real sick, going to be operated on today. We talked on the phone last night and he said his aunt Elaine's there. He wasn't in school today, and he won't be coming tomorrow."

"Did he say anything about the letter? Did you ask him?"

"No to both. Listen, Maizy, don't expect anything of him right now. His pa might die. He's got a lot on his mind." Fred finished the last of his milk and stuffed what was left of his lunch back in the bag. "I just came to tell you I had no news about the letter. I knew you'd be wondering."

Sure, she was wondering. Did Zane read her letter or not? And now, even if he read it, his pa was in the hospital and she wouldn't get to see Zane for a long time. She was on her own. But if you love a person, you can wait until they're ready. She'd wait forever for Zane.

"Fred, I gotta tell my pa. The clinic says so. Miss Adams wants to see him. Or they'll call the child welfare guys and they'll make me go to a home."

"Want me to be with you when you tell him?"

"Let him think it's your baby, you mean? Zane wouldn't go for that."

"No," he said. "Not to tell him that." Was she crazy to think such a thing? "Just to make sure he don't hit you again."

"What if he throws me out?" She wiped at her tears with the dishtowel.

"You could stay at my house. My ma would take you in. She did it for Flora at the hotel. Kept her until she had the baby."

"Then what happened?"

"Flora gave it up for adopting. She'd intended to do that all along."

"I'm not giving my baby up."

"I didn't say you were. Just, my ma would help you. She'd take Joey, too, for that matter."

Fred wasn't sure his ma could do it. She had a hard time making enough to pay the rent and feed the two of them. But he thought she'd find a way. She always did when someone needed help.

"Pa would never pay her for keeping us."

"She doesn't ask for money. Just does stuff because it needs to be done."

He was on his feet, ready to leave. "Think it over."

"Fred, you are such a good guy. But first I got to talk to Pa. Alone, unless Zane would come."

"Well, good luck. You can come by the store if you really need to." He put his hand gently on her stomach. "You look good, Maizy. I'm real sorry about all your trouble." He picked up her hand and kissed it.

"Don't tell your ma yet, Fred."

CHAPTER 25

Maizy

It was November when the first snow came.

Supper was over, and Maizy folded the dishtowel and returned it to its hook. She stood at the kitchen window over the sink, staring at the snow. The big, slow-falling flakes had a light of their own, looked like silver chips floating in the dark. There was something so quiet about snow, she thought. The quietness crept into the house, hushing its ordinary noises. Joey was in bed. He'd be so excited to see the snow in the morning.

Pa was reading the paper in the living room. Probably later he'd go out for a few hours. In the bathroom near the kitchen, she pulled a wet brush through her hair, threw cold water on her face, and checked her blouse to see if there were any spots. It gaped between the buttons. *The doc at the clinic said I have to watch what I eat for the baby's sake,* she told herself. She switched off the light and made her way into the living room.

She hadn't planned what she would say to Pa, she just couldn't think how to put it, but the words would find themselves. She was nervous about how Pa would take it. But no matter, he had to be told and she couldn't wait for Zane any longer.

"Pa, can I talk to you?" He groaned. He didn't like to be interrupted when he was reading the front page.

"You need more money for the house?" He didn't look up.

"No. It's not the house."

"Joey? He need shoes, clothes? Speak up, Maizy. You want a new dress?" He folded the paper in half, laid it on his lap, and dug in his back pocket for his wallet.

"It's not money, Pa. Can we just talk for a few minutes?"

Pa sighed. "Well, what?" They never talked, unless it was about the house or Joey. Pa knew nothing about Maizy's life; it seemed like he thought if he kept her and Joey fed and warm, it was all he had to do as a pa.

"How old was Ma when you got married?"

"Why you want to know?" He peered at her over the top of his glasses. Watched her as she went to sit on the couch opposite his chair. She smoothed back her hair, pulled her blouse straight, wet her lips.

"I don't remember much about Ma. Joey don't know anything. Kids want to know about their ma."

"Well, she was sixteen. I was seventeen. Most of our friends was getting hitched. In the mountains, we married young. Boys left school and worked on their pa's farm or in the mines."

"But not you?"

"No. I worked in my pa's farm store. When Patty got pregnant with you, we decided to come to Chicago. Stupid kids. We thought I could earn more and it'd be more fun living in a city."

"Didn't you want me to be born?"

"Wasn't about *you* being born. We just wasn't ready for a baby."

"But you loved me, you and Ma?"

" 'Course we did. Why you asking all this?"

"Just want to know. Am I anything like Ma?"

Her pa laughed. "Well, maybe inside. You got my looks mostly, but her ways. She was a kind person; patient, you could say. She was the prettiest girl in town, everybody said so."

Maizy had a picture of her ma, only one, a colored picture taken on her wedding day. She was standing in front of a blue painted door, next to a wild rose arbor, the roses in full bloom. She wore a long white dress, with blond curls spilling down past her shoulders, and a crown of pink rosebuds. She smiled, but her blue eyes looked scared. She looked like a young girl going on a journey, not sure of where she was going or if it was safe. Joey had her looks, with blond hair and blue eyes. "Did you love her a lot?"

"Didn't have much time for loving," Pa said. He took off his glasses and polished them with the hem of his shirt. "I worked all I could, she took care of the other things till she got sick."

Maizy remembered thinking of her ma that way, never having time. She was like a wind, sweeping through the house, one room to the other, her short blond hair always in a tangle, wearing her nightgown until she had to dress for shopping. There was the time before Joey, when her ma would stop her housework and play with her. They rolled in the grass with the neighbor's puppy and sprinkled each other with the hose. They laughed so much, and the dog ran around them barking as if he were laughing, too. They walked to the lake and sat on the stones, watching the water. In winter, they made snowmen with carrot noses. After Joey came, her ma didn't play anymore. When she wasn't sick or taking treatments, she took care of Joey. Neighbors came in most every day to help.

"You're my big girl," she remembered her mama saying. "You help me so much. Clean up the house before Pa gets home," she'd tell Maizy, and she remembered going from room to room picking up clothes and toys.

"But did you love her?" Maizy persisted. "Even if things were hard?"

"Why you asking all these questions?" Pa, getting impatient, started to unfold his paper. "Not thinking of getting married, are you?"

"Yes, Pa." Her heart was in her throat. Her body stiffened against the expected slap. "I'm getting ready to get married. I'm older'n Ma was," she added, anticipating a possible objection.

Pa took off his glasses and pinched the bridge of his nose. He closed his eyes and leaned his head back against the chair.

"What about Joey?"

She let out the breath she'd been holdng. He wasn't going to hit her.

"I'll always take care of Joey. I promised you."

"So who you planning on marrying? That Fred Fink kid? I thought he was queer."

"He's not queer, Pa, far's I know. He's my best friend. But he's not the one."

Her pa replaced his glasses and looked her up and down. She ran her hands down her front, pulling the bottom of her shirt taut over her jeans.

"Who, then?"

"Zane Caruthers."

"The minister's boy?" Pa laughed. "Are you crazy? What'd he be marrying you for?" Once again he ran his eyes over her body, not laughing now. "Did he knock you up?" His hands went to the arms of his chair as if he was getting up. His eyes narrowed to steel slits. Pa knew Zane like everyone else in the neighborhood did, ever since he was a little kid.

"Pa, just listen to me." Her voice was strong, surprising her. "Zane and I are in love. We're going to have a baby. I already went to the clinic doctor and it's true. And we're gonna get married. I can live here if you'll let me, until the baby's born"—she rushed her words to keep him from interrupting—"and Zane graduates and gets a job. Then if you want, I'll move out. Zane will find us a place. I'll take Joey with me or come here and take care of him. And do all the cooking and laundry and housework like I always do."

There. It was out. She hadn't planned any of it, but it seemed like a good idea to tell him now, before she got any bigger, and in time for the meeting at the clinic.

Pa slumped back in his chair. He looked old, with lines on his thin face she'd never noticed. His hair was getting

155

gray. His tired eyes glared at her. He wasn't going to hit her. Instead, he looked like he'd been hit himself.

"Got it all figgered out, have you?"

"The doctor says the baby's coming in April, just before Zane graduates."

"And what makes you think he's going to marry you and not go to college? The minister's kid? Does he even know about the baby?"

Now it was Maizy's turn to sigh. "Zane's pa is very sick in the hospital. I haven't had a chance to tell him yet. But he loves me. He said so. And when he knows about the baby, he'll want to get married. We both want the baby." Hard as she tried, she couldn't make her voice sound convincing.

Pa got up and went to sit near Maizy on the couch, facing her. He put a hand on her knee. Her father's touch. She couldn't remember the last time he'd touched her except when he'd hit her, the day the baby was started. It was so unexpected, seemed to her so tender that it brought tears. She tried to blink them back.

"Honey," Pa said, "I ain't been a real good pa to you and Joey. Since Patty died, I sort of put you in her place, to take care of things at home while I worked to keep us going. I forgot you were only a little girl yourself, only eight years old, and trying to be a ma to Joey, but still needing a ma yourself."

Maizy covered her face, but she couldn't hold back the tears that wet her fingers.

"I've been happy, Pa. I love Joey and you, and I'm happy taking care of you both. I want you to love our baby, and Zane, too."

"Maizy, listen to me. You can't have this baby." He'd gone back to his chair, but he didn't pick up the paper. Instead he lit his pipe.

A coldness washed over Maizy and she shivered.

"Pa, I always minded what you said. I done my best to be a good girl. But I tell you, I am not going to kill this baby. I'm going to get it born, and Zane and me are going to get married."

"I wouldn't tell you to kill the baby. Your ma and I, we don't believe in killing babies. We'd've had Joey even if we'd known he wasn't gonna be right. Here's what we'll do, Maizy. You'll have the baby, and we'll find a place to have it adopted. A good young family, who can give it things you can't."

"Pa, Zane won't want it that way. We want our baby."

"Tell you what, honey. If that boy comes here and says he wants to marry you, if he does it, official, and real soon, you can do what you want. But I'm warning you, he won't. His pa won't let him. He'll go off to college, and you won't see him again. When the baby's born, we'll find a good home for it. Will you go along with that?"

Maizy nodded. She'd managed to stop crying. A small pebble was growing into a rock in her chest, threatening to choke off her breath. She wiped her face with a tissue she had in her pocket.

Pa was so good, being reasonable and fair. Not getting mad. If he was right, and Zane didn't want her and the baby, she would have to give it up. There was no way she could go to work and take care of Joey and the baby, all by herself.

But in her heart, she still hoped that she was right this one time. That Zane would want her and his baby.

Her pa put his glasses in their case, put down his pipe, and rose from his chair.

"I'm going out for some air," he said. "Check on Joey and leave your door open when you go to bed so you'll hear if he wakes up."

"You don't have to tell me that," she said. "I always do it, all the time."

CHAPTER 26

Fred

Dear Fred,

I never see you anymore so I am writing you a letter to tell you what is happening to me. I hope all my spelling is right. I am using a dictionary for some of the words. I never was so good in spelling.

You said I will never see Zane again, but I think you are wrong. Love will find a way. It says that in books and magazines. And I believe it. If Zane has trouble now, it will make him feel better to know his baby is growing every day. My ma said, when Joey was just born, that babies are good luck. It was not so for her because she died, but it is a true saying for most people.

Fred, I told Pa about the baby. I could do it because of what you said, that I could come to your ma if he threw me out. And Joey, too. I was plenty scared. But I had to tell him because of the social worker.

He did not get mad like I thought. He did not hit me. I could tell he was disappointed in me, but he was great. Like you, he said that Zane would not marry me. He does not want to kill the baby, but said I have to give it away when it is born. Fred, I do not want to do this. But if you and Pa are right about Zane, I would have to get a job to pay for the baby. I do not think I can do this and take care of Joey and the house and everything. So if Zane does not want me and the baby, I will have to give it away.

But Fred, I will not give it to strangers even if they seem nice. How will I know the baby will be taken care of as it should? I have decided I will give my baby to Anna Carney and Josef, her husband, if they will take it. They are the ones who were the parents of Marta, the little girl who got killed and her hand is missing. Do you remember when it was in the Tribune?

Anna said the police are still looking for the killer. She said if they could find the hand that was missing when they found Marta, it could help them to find the killer. I hope they will find the killer, but even if they do, it cannot bring Marta back. Anna is so sad. And Josef looks every day for the hand.

Anna said he walks on the rocks near the lake where they found Marta's body. Josef says the lake will give back the hand, and that Marta cannot rest without it. I do not believe this and Anna does not either. But every day he looks. I am sad for them. I think if I give them my baby, they will be happy again. Anna said Josef wants to go back to Libra, Kentucky, where they lived before Chicago, but they won't go till the hand is found.

After my talk with Pa, I asked Anna if she would take my baby and she cried. First she said no, I must keep it, but

I told her how it is. She said it will make her want to live again if she has this baby. She has to ask Josef, but she knows he will say yes and will love the baby. They will take it to Libra, where some of their family is, and it will have a happy life. They are good people. I will never see my baby again, but I want it to have a good life and not go to strangers.

I am sorry this is such a long letter, but I want you to know how you helped me by saying I could go to your ma. And Joey, too. It was very nice, and you are the kindest boy I know, Fred. And your ma, too. I wish I had a ma to tell me what to do.

If you hear about Zane, I hope you will tell me. I still love him, but I am not so very sure if he loves me. I wonder how it would be if I loved you instead of Zane. I mean, I love you, but not that way.

Your friend, Maizy

Ma gave me the letter when I got home from work last night. First letter I ever got in the mail. I took it to my room, knowing Ma would want to know what it was about, but I didn't want to tell her until I knew myself.

It was from Maizy. I read it twice over. It's a good letter, no mistakes, far as I could see. I felt bad I didn't go see her to find out if she told her pa and how he took it. But when I get out of work, it's late and her pa might be home.

But I'd been thinking about her a lot. So I sat down right away and answered her letter.

Dear Maizy,

I was happy to get your letter. It's good that your pa knows about the baby and didn't get mad. Maizy, I think he is right, that you should give the baby away to a good home, where it will have a pa and a ma to take care of it.

Zane has not been to school for a long time, over a week. I called him up and he said his pa is very sick and his aunt Elaine is there. She is nice to him. They go to see his pa in the hospital every day, and the church people go too, and they bring food to their house. Miss Verner is not there anymore, either.

Zane does not know what will happen, if his pa gets well or if he dies. He can't talk or move anymore.

I do not think Zane could be a pa for the baby. Even if he wants to, he can't. The Rev had a stroke after he was operated on for his heart, and can't work in the church anymore. They will all go to live with his aunt and uncle in Iowa, Zane said. So you must forget about Zane for now, except to pray for him and the Rev.

It is a good idea to give the baby to Marta's mother. She will love it and her husband will too. Maybe they can have more babies later, to give it brothers or sisters.

Maizy, this is very important. You said Anna's husband goes to the lake to look for the hand. Is he a tall man with dark hair? Ask Anna if you don't know. I saw a man looking for something when I was at the lake, and I think it could be him. I will go there again and see if he is there. I can't tell you how, but if it is the man, I can help him.

You can come to the store where I work if you don't stay long.

Yours Truly,
Fred Fink.
P.S. If I ever loved a girl, it would be you.

I put the letter in an envelope and got on my bike to take it to Maizy's mailbox. It was late when I got there, and her house was dark. Then I rode past the house where the girl Marta was killed. It was dark, too. But Josef and Anna were sitting on the step wrapped in blankets. Not talking, just sitting there. The porch light was on, and I could see their faces. The man was the same one I saw at the lake looking for something.

I will get the hand for him.

CHAPTER 27

Fred

The day after I brought my letter to Maizy was Saturday. I hated to ask my boss if I could take off from bagging for the morning because of Saturday being a busy time, and I didn't want to get fired. But I had something important I needed to do. I rode my bike to the lake. I was going to stay until the man looking for the hand showed up. I had to be sure I knew what he was looking for before I did what I'd planned.

It started out to be a nice day, cold, but with sunshine. I passed the minister's house, but no one was around. Zane's car wasn't in the driveway, so maybe he got the keys back and went to the hospital to see his pa. One of our teachers who goes to the United Church of God, the Rev's church, tells us every day how the minister is doing and it isn't good. Last I heard, it sounded like he is on the way out.

It must be a hard time for Zane. I wanted to see him, but if I did, I wouldn't know what to say. My ma said I should send him a friendship card, but I didn't do it yet.

I got to the rocks along the lake and a wind came up

and started to blow big gray balloonlike clouds across the sky. The water was dark with patches of light, and heavy waves were beginning to come in, almost up to the rocks. If they splash on the rocks, it's dangerous to be there. You could get washed out into the water and carried by the undertow, way out past where you could swim back. I put my bike between two rocks above the water and climbed to a high place. I stood there facing the lake, my arms stretched out, my face in the wind, and I let it blow against me, splashing me with water cold like chips of ice on my face and hands. I opened my mouth and some of the ice chips came in and melted on my tongue. I didn't even feel cold. Must be how a bird feels, flying against the wind. Then the wind started to take my breath away and I climbed down. My jacket and hair were wet, and I suddenly felt real cold.

The guy won't come in this kind of weather, I thought, and I started to get my bike to go back. But then there he was, too far down on the rocks to be safe, looking into the lake.

"Hey," I yelled to him, to tell him to come up. I guess he didn't see the signs saying DANGER, KEEP OUT. He didn't hear me on account of the wind. He should've had sense enough to know it's dangerous. But he was pushing against the wind, his hair blowing all over his face, bending down, looking in the water. I couldn't just leave him there to get pulled into the lake and drown, so I had to climb down to where he could hear me yelling.

"Hey, mister!" I shouted.

He must've heard me, because he looked up.

"Come on up," I hollered, making motions with my arms. "It's dangerous."

"I'm okay," he shouted back. "Let me be."

I climbed down a little more, thinking, *This is stupid*. But if I went for help, he'd be washed away before I got back.

"Come on," I hollered. "Please come up. Or I gotta come down there and make you, and we could both drown."

Was I crazy, talking to a man like he was a boy, and like he'd listen to me anyway? But to my surprise, he started climbing up the rocks to where I was. I scuttled up higher and he came to where I was.

"What do you want?" he asked me.

"Nothing," I said. "Just, it's awful dangerous down there. Didn't you see the sign?"

"Why should you care what I, a stranger, will do?"

Good question. Why should I care? I guess I didn't think of why. I just cared. Maybe 'cause I knew what he was looking for. Or I thought I did.

"I saw you before. You seemed to be looking for something. I come here a lot. Maybe I can help you look."

"No," he said. "No one helps me. I do not want it."

He had a funny way of talking, like someone from another country. That made me sure he was Josef, the man Maizy told me about in the letter.

"Well," I said, "we should get away from here. You won't find anything today." It had started to rain, big fat drops, cold as ice. Josef was following me up the rocks. I got my bike and both of us climbed down, away from the lake to the strip of ground on the edge of Sheridan Road.

"Sir," I said, "is your name Josef Carney?"

He squinted at me, pushed his straggly hair off his face, and zippered his jacket up to the neck before answering.

"You know me?"

"You live on Kenmore. I've seen you around."

I didn't want to say anything about his little girl. It might make him mad, or think I was prying in his business.

"Yes. I am Josef Carney."

The traffic light changed and we both started across Sheridan Road. I got on my bike and soon passed him. Without looking back, I waved.

Now I knew who he was and what he was looking for. I had to find a way to deliver the hand to him. I could dig it up from under the floorboard in the shack and just bring it to his house: "Here's the hand you've been looking for." But that would be so gross. No, I'd just get the hand, put it in a box, and drop it off at his door some night, when no one was around. He would know it was his little girl's hand. I remembered the newspaper said there was a ring on one of the fingers, and Marko mentioned the ring—and the hunk of hair in the hand. But even without the ring, he'd know. A man like that would know his kid's hand, even if it was rotted. Maybe he'd suspect I was the one who brought it, but he wouldn't be able to prove it.

Riding home in the rain, I thought about what I was going to do. Maybe it was stupid. What if he took it to the police and somehow they found out I brought the hand to his house? They might think I killed the kid, or had something to do with it. But I had to get the hand for him. It was the right thing to do, even with the risk.

I wished I could talk to someone about it. Not my ma,

because she would say to be careful not to do something that would get me in trouble. I thought of Zane, but his aunt was there, and she didn't know anything about the hand. When I got home, I took a hot shower and put soup on the stove for lunch. Ma was working on Saturdays for over-time. After I ate the soup, I knew what I was going to do about the hand. But first I had to get back to my job.

CHAPTER 28

Zane

Zane pulled his car into the driveway, turned off the ignition, and sat staring at the lake. The sun glinted on the surface in tiny pinpoints of light, like the graphite specks on sidewalks. But no warmth came from the November sun, and Zane shivered. With the heater off, the car soon grew cold. He sighed, pulling himself out of the trance induced by the dancing light. A numbing tiredness seemed to creep over him every day, from the moment he got out of bed.

He had a bag of groceries to bring into the house for Aunt Elaine. He'd go inside, drink a glass of milk, and then get back in the car and drive somewhere—maybe nowhere. Just drive.

Aunt Elaine said he didn't have to go to school, that he'd be finishing high school in Iowa anyhow, because even if his dad got well from his stroke, he'd need full-time care for the rest of his life. That meant giving up his ministry, and both of them going to Iowa to live with her and Uncle Leroy. At first, he'd dreaded that happening, but it turned out it wouldn't be so bad. Aunt Elaine said he could go to Iowa State University in Ames after he graduated from high school. She'd gone there herself and knew they had a good art department.

She'd come across his cartoons when she went into his room one day to open a window and had seen the sketchbook on his desk.

"These are good," she'd said, surprising him. He'd thought she'd get mad like his dad did, whenever he caught him wasting time on what he considered kid stuff. To his father, drawing was for either kids or drifters.

"Are you planning to be an artist?"

"I want to," he'd said, "but Dad—"

"Wants you to go into the ministry. Am I right?"

"Yeah, but—"

"You don't want to. Zane, a person can't be good at something he doesn't like."

Zane was relieved. His aunt was on his side! But what if his father made him promise? You have to keep your promise to a dying person, don't you?

Aunt Elaine was the one good thing to happen to him in a long time. Zane'd expected to hate her. But it turned out she was different from what he expected, and very different from his dad. She spoke in short sentences, as if she was in a hurry to get things said, instead of lecturing like his father. It seemed like she had everything all planned out. He'd've thought this would make him mad, not being consulted on what was going to happen in his life. But actually, it was a relief. He hated discussions with adults. They just bored you with reasoning, when they'd already decided what they were going to do anyway, and were only talking to you about it to make it seem you were in on it. His aunt didn't *discuss,* and that was okay with him. There was nothing he could do about the things that were happening anyhow.

She seemed to like him, too. Maybe because she had no kids herself.

His aunt wasn't a looker. Medium height like his dad, but heavier than he'd been when he was well. Dressed plain, but okay to go with her short brown hair and glasses. Treated him with respect, unlike his father.

He brought the groceries into the kitchen. Aunt Elaine was at the table, drinking coffee.

"Eat some breakfast," she said. "Want me to fix an omelet?"

"No, thanks." Zane poured the glass of milk. If she hadn't been there, he'd have drunk it out of the carton, like he did to make Miss Verner mad. His aunt had fired the housekeeper right away, and she'd let a lot of the household rules go by, but he didn't think she'd go for him drinking out of the carton.

"I'm going out. Okay?"

"Be back soon. I want you to take me to the hospital in a while, so that your father won't be alone too long. You can spend an hour with your dad and then leave, as long as you come back and pick me up at six tonight."

His dad was in a coma. He was so thin, his body hardly showed under the sheet. He looked like he was asleep, but without the softness of a sleeping face, he looked perfectly blank, with no expression at all. The frown lines he always had were gone, like they'd been erased. He was nearly as white as the sheet, even his lips. His nostrils were the only color in his face, thin, smoke-colored slits. His hair, longer now than he wore it, looked like summer-bleached grass. He got oxygen through a tube in his nose, and food from a tube in his arm. His arms, bare under the hospital gown, were thin as pencils, his fingernails long and clean.

"Talk to him," his aunt said. "Maybe he can hear you."

It seemed weird, like talking to a dead person. And getting close to him, there was that smell of hospital, and something else, sour and bitter. Must be what death smelled like.

"Dad? I'm here. It's me, Zane, your son. It's okay, Dad. You'll get better. I say prayers for you every day. Okay, Dad?"

He didn't know what more to say, what he was supposed to say. He hadn't been able to say "I love you." It was in his mind, but it just wouldn't come out. He couldn't remember ever having said it to his dad. He stood as close to him as he could without touching the bed. Once he thought he saw an eyelid flicker. But the eye didn't open. His aunt stroked his dad's face, pushed back his hair, held his hand. But Zane couldn't bring himself to touch him.

He went to sit in a chair near the window, and his aunt sat on the bed and talked to her brother as if he could hear her, telling him about the house, and things in the past. She told him a lot of times that they loved him, her and Zane.

After what seemed like hours, Aunt Elaine said, "You can go now, honey. Come back at six. You'll say good night to him and we'll go home." She called him "honey" and he didn't mind, long as no one heard.

He got into the car in the parking lot and turned up the heater. He was always cold.

Everything felt unreal. The sky was a phony blue, like in a comic strip. Cars that seemed like toys moved alongside him, passed him with their honking horns that sounded muted and far away.

Middle of a day in November, and he wasn't in school. Didn't have to be anywhere, or doing anything. The street was slick with melted snow. In the next lane was the salt truck, doing its job. But all that salt didn't help the tires any.

He should be thinking about his dad, lying there like he's dead. Did he think about anything? Did he hear them talking to him? Was a coma kind of like practicing to die? If they pricked him with a pin, would he feel it? His jumbled thoughts reminded him of a kaleidoscope, with its always changing shapes and colors.

I should feel sad, Zane thought. But he didn't feel a damn thing, only empty. He didn't even realize he was driving the car. Where was he going? Better snap out of it, before he had an accident.

Make a plan. He'd drive over to Kenmore, go to the delicatessen for a sandwich and some Coke. He was hungry. The kids would be at school or working. *That's good,* he thought. He didn't want to see anyone he knew.

Maizy. She might be in the store. He couldn't face her, and what he did to her at the shack. Her letter that he hadn't read. The cruddy things he'd said about her. He'd treated her bad, just for liking him.

He wouldn't go to the grocery store. Couldn't risk seeing her. There were candy bars in the glove compartment. With one hand on the wheel, he dug in, got a Baby Ruth, tore the wrapper off with his teeth, and devoured it.

Without knowing how he got there, he felt the wheels of the car stuttering over the rubble of the empty lot. The car came to a stop in front of Z's—exactly where he'd parked the day he brought Maizy there. He knew the spot because it was on a broken cement slab under a tree, where the car would be invisible from the street.

It was freezing cold in the shack. It looked like no one had been there in a long time. He sat on the edge of the couch. The fabric was damp and smelled like wet dog. On the table was a box of charcoal Fred must have brought when he came to work on his cartoons.

A long time ago, when he'd found the junky, wrecked shack in the empty lot behind the billboard, he'd got the idea to have a hideout, thought of calling it Z's. He got some of the guys from school to come there by offering them a private place to hang out, to smoke, to bring girls if they wanted. Thought it would make him important in their eyes, not just a rich kid from Sheridan Road, slumming it in their neighborhood.

The guys never thought of it as anything special. They probably had their own places where he was never invited. Marko buried the hand there because it was the least likely place anyone would find it and get him in trouble. After that, they all lost interest, dropped him. All except for Fred.

Fred was his only friend. A feeling of loss came over him, thinking of Fred. The first real feeling he'd had since his dad got sick. He hadn't wanted to see him though, to have Fred feel sorry for him and all that shit. But now he wished Fred was in the shack with him, sitting at the table, sketching a comic strip.

He felt the dampness of the couch right through his jeans. What if Maizy happened to walk in right this minute, bringing cookies like she'd done once before? He could see her, her mess of butter-colored hair tied back with a string, freckles sprinkled over her nose like salt, eyes blue as the lake on a sunny day. She'd be wearing coveralls and a sweater. Her good-smelling body, clean and warm as a pillow. She'd sit down close to him on the couch, and without saying a word, take him in her arms and hold him.

He noticed that the loose floorboard where the hand was buried looked different, as if someone had pried it open and then pushed it back. Maybe a dog had got into the shack and smelled it, maybe dug it up and took it away, ate it, even. Gross! He didn't care if it was still there or not.

He went to the back of the shack and looked out the window at the drab empty lot, the dried-out grass, a couple scrubby trees. Just dreariness all around. He shivered, got back in the car, ate two more candy bars, and headed for the hospital. It was time to pick up his aunt. Say good night to his dad.

CHAPTER 29

Zane

Zane drove into the hospital parking lot at five forty-five in the evening. A wet wind blew snow flurries past the parking lot lights, the luminous chips disappearing as they landed on the wet asphalt. Afternoon visiting hours were over at six, and the lot was nearly empty. He pulled the hood of his jacket over his head and jammed his hands into his pockets. But he didn't hurry across the lot into the warm lobby. He dreaded going inside.

Pushing through the revolving door, he exchanged the clean frosty smell of the night for the sharp, antiseptic smell of the lobby.

The elevator, already loaded with an attendant and his unconscious patient on a gurney, stopped to admit Zane and three other visitors. He stared at the floor to avoid looking at the sick guy.

He got off on six and saw, down the hall, that the door of his father's room was closed. Aunt Elaine always insisted on it being open. His heart plunged. Something was wrong. Fear knotted his stomach. He felt dizzy, and vomit burned his throat. What was behind the closed door?

He stopped in the men's room, peed, washed his hands, and cleaned under his nails with a toothpick he found in his pocket, taking his time, dreading going to his father's room. *I don't want him to die,* he thought.

Then he walked down the brightly lit corridor, his heart quaking, the glare burning his eyes, to room 610. He forced himself to lift his leaden arm to the doorknob, then changed his mind and knocked. Immediately, as if she'd been standing there waiting, his aunt opened the door.

"He passed at three," she said. "Come in and say goodbye to your father."

At the bedside, Zane looked at the first dead person he'd ever seen, a wax dummy that in no way resembled his dad. He had no feeling for this body, no pity or fear. His mind was white, empty. He had nothing to say.

"Come on," his aunt said. She didn't make a fuss about saying goodbye to his dad. "Let's go have some dinner. I'll have to sign some papers later, then we'll go home. Tonight we'll decide about the funeral."

"Could you decide?" Zane said. "I don't know anything about funerals."

He supposed he'd feel something later, when he got used to his dad being dead.

They left the hospital and Zane drove, following his aunt's directions to the Cosmopolitan Inn. They ordered steaks. Aunt Elaine poured them each a glass of wine from the carafe she ordered. The waiter didn't say anything about

Zane being old enough to drink it. Zane was surprised how hungry he was. They ate slowly, didn't talk. While she paid the check, he went to get the car from the valet.

Zane couldn't shake the feeling of being out of his body, of watching this guy get into the car, put the key into the ignition, start the car.

"Feel okay to drive?" his aunt asked when she got in.

"Yeah, sure," the boy behind the wheel said. And then he was in front of his house, but how had he gotten there?

Entering the house, he suddenly connected with reality. This was his house, and his room, with all his things, was upstairs. The familiarity calmed him. Everything was as it had been that afternoon, when he'd driven Aunt Elaine to the hospital and himself to the shack, to Z's. But somehow, now everything was different.

"Sit here with me for a few minutes," his aunt said. "I want to tell you what'll be happening the next few days, and then you can go to your room if you want to."

Zane sighed. He didn't want to hear about the next few days. And all the days to come after them. He felt so tired. So empty.

"There are things we have to do for your father," Aunt Elaine was saying. "Things a family must do when they lose a loved one."

"Please," Zane said. "Can't you take care of it?"

"We'll do them together," she said. "We're his family."

❖

In the next days, Zane and his aunt selected a coffin for his father. They brought clothes to the undertaker for the Rev to wear in his coffin, and the whole time, Zane felt like a robot. He couldn't find any feelings in himself, and he wanted only to sleep. He did what he was told, and he said yes to everything.

Before the funeral, Zane and his aunt went to the church for "the viewing," as Aunt Elaine had called it. There they sat for hours, with prayer books open on their laps, as the church members came to pay their respects to his father, their pastor. They walked past the coffin with murmurs and sad faces, some hugging Zane and saying they were sorry for his loss. He didn't know what to say to them, or even what he was supposed to do. Some of them stayed for a while, praying silently in the pews.

"You can talk to your father," Aunt Elaine said. It seemed like something you were supposed to do. But the man in the coffin was not his father, and Zane had nothing to say to him.

"Go out for a walk," his aunt suggested. "Or take a ride in your car." He did, and when he returned to the church, people were still coming to visit his father.

❖

Later, the house was filled with food that church members brought for the family. You could smell it before you even opened the front door. And each time someone came in with a platter, Aunt Elaine said, "Thank you. So thoughtful of you."

❖

"The funeral is tomorrow," his aunt said. "You and I will be the only family there. Uncle Leroy can't come— he's needed at the store."

It was only three days since his father had died. But to Zane, it felt a lot longer.

"After we say goodbye to your father's friends and congregants from the church, we'll be packing to leave."

"I really can't get used to the idea of leaving, Aunt Elaine."

Zane had lived in the house all his life, and even though he'd been happy at the prospect of going to art school in Iowa, it now dawned on him that he really was leaving the only home he'd ever known.

"The house belongs to the church, Zane. When they knew your dad was sick and had to resign, they appointed a new minister. He's taken over services already, but he's been waiting to move in while all this was going on, while your father was dying. So now we're going home, to Iowa, where you're going to live—with us. We'll have your things shipped."

Aunt Elaine spoke to him slowly, as if she was giving Zane time to let it all sink in, about leaving Chicago. About going home to Iowa.

Just like that, Zane thought. *"Home to Iowa?"* Iowa wasn't home. He belonged here, in Chicago with his dad. *I can't just go away and leave him here alone,* he thought.

And who am I without him?

CHAPTER 30

The Funeral

Zane

Zane and his aunt sat in the front pew, about six feet from the open coffin, where the dead man lay. His father was dressed in one of his Sunday suits, waxy hands crossed on his chest, the body covered from the waist down by a blanket of white roses. Candles burned, their flames trembling. Masses of flowers were banked behind the casket, and beside it was the pulpit.

Sunrays streamed through the stained-glass windows, ribbons of red and blue, filling the church with a wavy, underwater light. The smell of candle wax, flowers, and perfume, along with the presence of the dead, gave the place a creepy feeling.

Zane's head ached, his chest felt heavy, he couldn't take a deep breath. He thought of excusing himself to go to the bathroom, but someone had just entered the pulpit. A cleric wearing a heavy black robe placed an open Bible on the stand and switched on a small reading light. *The new minister,* Zane thought. Younger than his dad, but with the same serious, tense look of every minister he'd ever seen.

The new minister was speaking of Reverend Caruthers, a man of God dedicated to his congregation. Zane tried to pay attention.

Good works, leadership, integrity. A pure man before God, loved and revered by his flock. A devoted father to his son, father and mother to Zane since his wife and the boy's mother had been taken from them.

Prayers were read from the Bible, and responded to with *amens.* The words flowed into one another, the words you say of the dead, even if you know nothing about the person.

Had this minister even seen his father alive? Would he still call him a good father if he knew about the silences between him and his son? The put-downs and the anger, because Zane wasn't good enough to be the minister's son? What if he knew about those pictures in the envelope in the drawer? Would a good man, a good reverend, keep dirty pictures of little girls? Zane wished he'd never found them.

Well, his dad was dead now, so what difference did it make that he'd never known Zane, never let him be who he was, never appreciated what he was good at, didn't know a thing about his life? Did it matter that he'd never hugged Zane, or told him that he loved him? Zane supposed it didn't—not anymore.

Why am I having these thoughts now? Zane asked himself. *Am I going crazy?*

Tears rolled down his cheeks. *Shit!* He was crying for himself, not for his dad. He covered his face with his hands.

Dad, I loved you! I loved you, only you never knew it, and now it's too late to tell you.

Maizy

Maizy asked her pa if he'd watch Joey for a few hours on Sunday. She wanted to go to the minister's funeral.

"What for?" her pa asked. "So you can cry over that phony?" He thought all church people were phonies. "Or so you can see your bastard's pa?"

That hurt Maizy. It wasn't the baby's fault that it wouldn't have a father. She already loved the baby inside her, and so did Joey.

"Can we keep it, Maiz?" Joey kept asking.

"No," she'd told him. "We can't take care of it."

"We can," Joey said. "I can help. I'll be the pa and get a job, and give you money to buy food for it. I can help you! Please, Maiz."

Joey didn't realize he was a reason she couldn't keep the baby—the main reason. If not for Joey, she could get a job and make enough to pay for someone to take care of the baby while she was at work. She knew she'd have a very hard time trying to take care of Joey and a baby and also work.

"It needs a real ma and pa, Joey. I'm giving it to people who will love it forever."

"I'll take Joey with me," Maizy said, when her pa said she couldn't go. "I'm *going* to the church." She didn't care if Pa hit her. This was one time she would do what she wanted. Zane was all alone, now that his pa was dead. He needed her.

"Joey stays here," her pa said. "Just don't be too long. Sunday's my only time off."

❖

Maizy sat in the back of the church, behind a pillar. She wanted to be invisible. By leaning over and looking past the pillar, she could see the minister, the coffin, and Zane in the front row. The flowers, the candlelight, the holy smell of the room, the rays of sunlight coming in from the widows in streams of purple and green and red, to Maizy made the church seem like a magical, mysterious world.

She listened to the flowing voice of the minister and thought, *You have to live a perfect life, be an unsoiled person, to have such words said about you*. She'd already lost her chance of being such a person, and she wondered if her baby had also lost that chance, about to be born to a damaged person like her.

When the prayers were over, the minister invited everyone to the cemetery for the burial, saying that the pall-bearers should meet the funeral car at the gates. She watched the people stream out of the church, many wiping their eyes. Zane stood by the casket looking at his father, probably saying goodbye. He looked so beautiful to her, his blond hair shining in the church light. In his black suit, he looked so young and thin, and alone. Her heart overflowed with love for him. She left her seat and walked down the aisle. Her black tent dress, which she'd bought at Sears with some of the leftover food money, the only black dress she'd ever owned, floated around her. She wanted to tell Zane she loved him, that he was not alone, and that she'd always be there for him.

When she got to the front of the church, she went to stand near Zane. She knew he wouldn't notice she was pregnant because of her tent dress, and besides, he wasn't looking at her.

But then she looked in the casket.

"*Oh, God!*" she cried. It was nearly a scream. She covered her mouth with both hands. Her head spun, and her heart felt like it would burst.

It was the man on Kenmore, the one in the business suit, same one he was wearing now. It was the man she'd seen in the park lavatory—with the little girl, who she now knew wasn't his little girl. But she must have been Marta.

Now it became clear to her. This was the man who'd killed Marta and cut off her hand, and then threw her in the lake. When she'd told Anna about seeing the girl with a man in the lav, Anna'd been sure it was Marta. She was right. The killer was Zane's father!

Maizy started to shake. She'd been too afraid to tell the police. If she hadn't been such a coward, and so afraid that the man would come after her—if she hadn't assured herself it was all right, that he was in there with the girl *when she knew it wasn't*—maybe Marta would still be alive.

I killed Marta, she thought, *or as good as did. I will go to hell.* She thought she would faint right there, in front of the coffin. She closed her eyes, took several deep breaths. Her mind went white with the terrible realization.

"What's the matter with you?" Zane said. "Didn't you ever see a corpse before?"

She forced herself to look away from the body in the coffin. She stared at Zane. "Is that your father?"

"Who'd you think it was?"

Then a man came to close the coffin.

Zane was pale as a sheet, with dark rings under his eyes. His father was dead, and she was *never* going to tell him, or anyone else, that he was *not* a man of God like the minister had said, or like Zane probably thought.

She wouldn't tell him that his father was going to hell. It would hurt Zane too much to know that. She was the only one who knew, and she'd never tell. Never, no matter how God punished her for keeping such a terrible secret.

Maizy put her arms around Zane, and held him tight against her as the men wheeled the coffin out of the church. She stroked his blond hair, and she felt his body relax into her for a moment, then stiffen again. His eyes were closed as if he wanted to shut out this terrible day. She thought she heard him say *I love you,* very softly in her ear. She thought she heard it. "I love you," she whispered to him, just before he pulled away from her. That made everything better for her, no matter what happened now.

"You don't belong here," he said. "Why'd you come?" There was pain in his eyes, but his voice was icy cold. Then he turned and followed the men wheeling the closed coffin.

Maizy sat down in the front pew where Zane had been sitting, to wait until her heart stopped thundering, until her legs felt steady enough to carry her home. Pa was waiting for her to get home and watch Joey so he could go to his friends at the park. They had a ball game every Sunday.

She'd never before known what it was to be so terribly sad, so hopeless. So alone.

But Zane said "I love you," she assured herself. She knew he did.

Fred

I was the first to leave the church after the funeral. Ma said I should go to the cemetery for the burial, that it was the right thing to do, so I hung around outside the church until the hearse left for the cemetery.

I biked to the cemetery and parked my bike in some bushes. There was a long open hole, and the casket was on a frame just above it. The people from the funeral were all there, everyone except Maizy. I looked for her, wanting to stand with her. She was at the funeral, sitting behind a pillar. So why didn't she come for the burial?

❖

The hearse arrived just after I got there. When the coffin was brought out, seven people came forward to wheel it to the burial place, six men and one boy—Zane. He wore a black suit, and his blond hair was slicked down. His face was white and blank as a sheet of paper. He must be hurting something terrible inside. I wanted to go over to him and put my arms around him. But he had to do this alone, bring his father to his grave.

❖

The minister said some prayers, and then they put the box in the earth. It was cold out and it seemed like his words were wrapped in the steam from his mouth. I could smell the cold wet earth from the mound of dirt standing near the grave. It waited to cover up the coffin when it was put down into the hole.

Everyone left when the prayers were over, except Zane and his aunt. And me, standing behind them. They stayed at the grave, she on one side, he on the other, like they were guarding it. Then she went to wait for him in the car, so I thought this would be a good time to speak to him, say I'm sorry about his pa. He was looking down at the grave; not crying, just staring—as if he wanted to jump in.

"Zane," I said, coming up to him and putting my hand on his shoulder. "Sorry about your pa. He was a good guy." I wanted to hug him, but I didn't dare.

"Yeah," Zane said. "I guess. Those pictures I showed you were never his."

Funny, we were thinking about the same thing.

"No way," I said.

❖

"Why aren't you eating?" Ma asked the night of the funeral. We'd sat down for dinner. And she'd made pot roast and mashed potatoes, my favorites.

"Zane's an orphan now," I said.

I told her he'd said he was going to Iowa to live with his aunt, and that she would let him go to college and study art.

"So you see," she said, "bad things sometimes lead to good things."

"Yeah," I said. "No way did he want to be a minister, like his pa had wanted."

"He seemed like a nice boy," Ma said. "You'll miss him."

She didn't know about Maizy being knocked up, or how Zane wouldn't even look at the letter she sent him. Or how he talked mean about her, when she never did anything but love him.

Ma didn't know about those pictures Zane stole from his pa. I wondered if he burned the pictures or put them back in his pa's drawer, to be found by whoever looked there. I groaned to myself, imagining what the church people would think of the holy reverend if they saw those pictures now.

But Ma was right. I'd miss Zane a lot. I loved him in a certain way I'd never loved anyone before. Nothing he did could change that, no matter how wrong it was.

But the reason I couldn't eat the pot roast Ma fixed for me, and the mashed potatoes—my favorite food—was because of something else my ma didn't know.

She didn't know that I'd brought the hand to Josef.

I'd left work a little early the day before the Rev's funeral, went to the shack, and dug up the hand. It was under the loose floorboard, just like Marko said. It was wrapped in rotting newspaper. The hand was decaying, smelled awful, and looked like it was all bones. But the ring was still on the finger, and two bony little fingers still held some hair. The pervert's hair.

With my gloves on, I scooped the hand from the hole in the ground, into a box I brought from home, then wrapped it in clean newspaper, as neat as I could. The hand looked so frail that it might break into a million pieces if you dropped it. It was creepy, and it bothered me something awful. I'd never touched a dead person before, never mind a dead, unattached hand. Then I biked to Josef's house, put it in front of the door, rang the bell, and scrammed.

I thought about how shocked Josef and his wife would be when they opened the box and saw a little dug-up hand. Would Josef just put it in Marta's grave, so she could be whole again, even though she was dead? Or would he give it to the police? The hair could help identify the killer. But that was up to Josef. I was out of it now. Done.

I tossed my gloves in the laundry hamper, but even after they were washed, I'd probably never wear them again. They'd been tainted by a dead hand.

I wondered if I did right, getting Josef that hand. Ma says it's how you mean what you do that counts, no matter how a thing turns out, and I only meant to help him.

No one would know I'd dug it up. Except Zane might guess, if he ever found out that the hand was gone from the shack.

But Zane wouldn't ever be at Z's again.

CHAPTER 31

The Aftermath

Chicago Tribune November 28:

A significant breakthrough has occurred in the ongoing investigation of the murder of five-year-old Marta Carney. The little girl's fully clothed body was found floating in Lake Michigan on June second. The right hand was missing. According to the coroner's report, the child had been raped and asphyxiated, and the hand severed after her death.

Marta was the daughter of Josef and Anna Carney, nee Karnofsky. The family came to Chicago over a year ago from Libra, Kentucky, where they'd lived since emigrating from Warsaw, Poland. When Carney identified the body, he told police that his daughter always wore a silver ring on the fourth finger of the missing severed hand.

Sometime last night, an unknown person left a box containing a decayed hand, a silver ring on the fourth finger, at Carney's door. This morning, Carney brought the box containing the hand to the Kenwood District police station, saying he hoped it would help them in finding Marta's killer.

"It is Marta's hand," Carney said. "See, she still wears her ring."

According to Detective Sergeant John Alvarado, who has been working on the case from the start, the hand is clenched in a fist, and holds a few strands of the probable murderer's hair.

In a statement to the Tribune, *Alvarado said: "In her struggle for survival, Marta pulled out a fistful of the murderer's hair and held it in a death grip. The killer, most likely afraid that the hair could be used to identify him, cut off the hand and disposed of it before dumping the body in the lake. The return of the hand could provide an important clue to the murderer's identity."*

Sergeant Alvarado has agreed to release the remains of the hand to Carney as soon as possible, to be placed in the tomb of the murdered child.

"Without her hand, Marta cannot rest," Carney stated.

Zane

It was Zane's last night in Chicago, the last night he'd sleep in the bed he'd slept in all his life. But though he was tired to the bone, he couldn't sleep. His father had been a silent man, but the house without his presence seemed like a body without a beating heart. It was spooky and foreign, and it didn't want him there.

In the morning he'd be leaving for Iowa with Aunt Elaine. He'd never have seen the article about the hand being returned to Josef Carney if he hadn't been tearing sheets of paper to wrap up his drawing supplies for shipping.

The headline caught his eye: CHILD'S HAND FOUND: A CLUE TO KILLER OF MARTA CARNEY?

He read the short article about the hand. He remembered reading about the girl being murdered last summer. She'd been five, about the age of some of the littlest girls in those terrible pictures in his father's drawer, the little girls who floated through his nightmares.

It was the same hand Marko had found in a garbage can, and that they'd buried under the loose board in the shack. He remembered the silver ring, and how the hand held some hair, some sandy-colored hair, about the same shade as his own.

Who'd dug it up? Only he and Fred and the guys who came to the shack knew it was there. Now the police had it, and they were sure to find the murderer. Probably some perverted drifter.

He remembered the hairs clutched in the hand. Ugh. It wasn't something he wanted to think about—not now, not ever.

Those hairs. Maybe they *would* identify the killer. They were just ordinary hairs, the color of straw. Lots of men had hair that color. His dad—his dad had that color hair. Could his dad—? Horrified at the thought, Zane bit down hard on his lip, bringing blood. God would punish him for thinking such a thing about the departed, about his own father.

I'm so mixed up, Zane thought. *This isn't the real me. I'm lost and I'll never be found.*

Maizy

Maizy wore the tent dress she'd worn to the funeral nearly every day now. Her stomach was getting so big, nothing else fit. The dress made her look even fatter than she was, but she thought it hid her pregnancy. The clinic doctor said she was in her fourth month, and the baby was doing well.

It had started to snow while she was walking Joey to school, and he'd wanted to go back home and play in it.

"You'll play in the snow at school," she told him. "Soon there'll be enough so you and your friends can make a snowman."

Back home, she was making the beds and remembering that she hadn't taken her vitamins when she heard Anna at the door.

"Maizy, Maizy!" she called. She seemed excited or upset. Maizy couldn't tell.

"Come in, Anna. You're covered with snow." She was surprised. Anna had never come to the house before. "I have hot coffee, and I'll make us some toast."

Anna hung her wet coat on the closet doorknob and followed Maizy to the kitchen. She was dressed as usual, as if she'd pulled her clothes off a rack at a thrift store, not caring what she looked like. Her face, wet from the snow, was extra pale today.

"Maizy." She spoke quietly now, almost in a whisper. "A miracle."

"A miracle?" Maizy handed her a kitchen towel to dry her face.

She knew the miracle had to do with Marta. Nothing else could make Anna look so agitated. She put her hands on her stomach and felt a flutter. The doctor had said she'd soon be feeling life.

"Marta's hand. It was in a box on our porch." Now tears were streaming down Anna's cheeks.

"Jesus Christ!" Maizy put a cup of coffee on the table in front of Anna and stared at her. Josef had searched and searched for the hand, and now someone had found it and brought it to him. It really *was* a miracle.

"Now Marta can rest. Josef says so."

"Oh, Anna. I'm glad for you," Maizy said, and covered Anna's hands with her own. "What about the police?" she asked. "Did Josef take it to the police? So they can find who killed Marta?"

"Yes. They will give it back when they finish. Maybe they find Marta's killer. In the hand was hair, the killer's hair."

Maizy's legs felt weak, as if they wouldn't hold her. She sat down quickly on a kitchen chair.

The killer's hair! It could never help them find the killer. I'm the only one who knows! Marta's killer will never be found, she thought. *He's under the ground forever, in his grave. I have to live with that secret for the rest of my life,* she thought.

"Who brought you the box?" she asked.

"No one knows," Anna said. "Why does it matter? Now we have her hand. Now Josef can stop walking every day near the lake in the cold and wind."

Fred knew about Josef looking for the hand in the lake.

Maizy remembered she'd told him in her letter. She was sure he was trying to help Josef, and had somehow found the hand. That was like Fred. He wouldn't want anyone to know he found it and brought it to Josef. And she'd never tell. Another secret to keep forever.

"When the police give it back, will you put the hand with Marta?"

"Yes. We will put it in the grave," Anna said. "Give it back to Marta."

She placed her hand on Maizy's stomach. Maizy was sure the baby could feel its heat through her skin.

"We wait for your baby. When she comes, we will take her back to Libra. It is a better place to live, for us. We want to call her Maizy if it's a girl."

When she'd offered them her baby, Anna said she'd have to ask Josef. And without hesitating, he told his wife he wanted the baby.

Maizy was glad her and Zane's child would have a good home forever, and be loved. Their baby would not be given to strangers.

She would never see it again, once it was born and Anna and Josef moved away. And Zane wouldn't ever know he had a child. This was sad, but nothing could be done about it. It was the best solution for all of them.

"I'll go home now," Anna said. "To be with Josef. He does not work today. But I wanted you to know."

She reached out and Maizy went into her arms. They held each other for a long time, too full of emotion for any words. Then Anna knelt, caressed the baby inside Maizy with both hands, and kissed it through the black tent dress.

After Anna left, Maizy wept for the baby she'd never get to know.

Fred

When I read the story in the paper about the hand and all, I felt weird. No one will ever know how it got to Josef. It's like I have a secret I need to keep forever. Should a kid my age have a secret like that?

Seems like I've collected a lot of secrets since moving to Kenmore. Like knowing who's the father of Maizy's baby. No one but me and her pa know who it is. Zane never found out, and Maizy didn't tell anyone else.

And there's another secret I'm keeping—the Rev's dirty pictures. The Rev's dead now, and only me and Zane know about those pictures. Maybe Zane burned them.

Another secret I'll keep forever, the worst one of all, is one I'll never know for sure if it's true. But I think I know who killed Marta: it was Zane's father, the Rev.

The hairs in the hand could be his. They were that same, dry-sand color. And he had those pictures of the little girls. Maybe Marta's picture was there. I never looked that closely.

If I told the police about finding the pictures in his briefcase, they might dig him up and check his hair. If it matched and they find out he did it, it could mess up Zane's life forever. *And* it would break his heart.

So I'm keeping mum. The Rev's dead anyway. He can't hurt anyone else, ever again.

❖

Maizy showed me a letter Zane wrote to her. She could hardly believe she got a letter from him. I memorized the words:

Dear Maizy,

I know you were always my friend, no matter what I did to you.

Lots of things I said, I didn't mean—it was just to make me feel big.

You see, I never felt like I amounted to much. Maybe I'll have a new life now, and be a better person. I hope you can forgive me.

Zane

"See?" She said, "It proves he loves me."

"How?" I asked. He didn't sign it, 'love.' "

"It's a code, because he's too shy to tell me in words. The first letters of the first three sentences, I, L, and Y, stand for 'I Love You.' "

How'd she figure that out? But I'm glad she thinks it, and I feel good about Zane for writing the letter. He doesn't know about the baby, and I don't think he ever will.

❖

It's almost Christmas, and seven months since Ma and I came to Kenmore. But it seems like I was never anywhere else but here, like I've known Zane and Maizy forever.

They've gotten to be the most important people in my life. They showed me who I am.

I love Zane in my own special way, and so does Maizy, in hers.

He'll be living far away soon, but I'll never forget the time we spent together. I'll always be a friend to Maizy, but I probably won't be seeing her much anymore. I'm not really interested in girls, and I don't want her to start thinking of me as a boyfriend. And if we pass each other on Kenmore, and we stop to talk, Zane's name might come up, or maybe it won't.

Z's is over. Zane meant the shack as a hangout, where his friends would come and do their thing. But mostly no one came. Those guys didn't care about Zane, or me, either. It wasn't really the hangout that he wanted it to be, just the invention of a kid who wanted a place where he could belong, with guys who'd be his friends. But it never worked out that way.

But to us three—me, Zane, and Maizy—Z's was a real place.

It's over now. We're all changed.

We're not those kids anymore.

Acknowledgments

My appreciation to Evelyn Fazio, my publisher, without whose patient help and encouragement this book would never have come forth.

And to the members of my workshops who believed in the book from the start, added encouragement to critique, and constantly kept me from getting carried away:

Jenny Gumpertz, Joanne Hardy, Harf Windsor, Jane Sutherland, Kathryn Jordan, and Margaret Seeley.

DATE DUE			

DEMCO